July Underwater

ZOE MAEVE

July Underwater
© Zoe Maeve Jenkins, 2022
First Edition
Printed by The Prolific Group, Winnipeg, MB, Canada

Library and Archives Canada Cataloguing in Publication
Title: July underwater / Zoe Maeve.
Names: Maeve, Zoe, author, artist.
Identifiers: Canadiana 20220147426 | ISBN 9781772620696 (softcover)
Subjects: LCGFT: Graphic novels.
Classification: LCC PN6733.M34 J85 2022 | DDC 741.5/971—dc23

Text from The Price of Salt © Estate of Patricia Highsmith
Text from To the Lighthouse © Estate of Virginia Woolf

Conundrum Press
Wolfville, Nova Scotia
www.conundrumpress.com

Conundrum Press acknowledges the financial support of the Canada Council
for the Arts, The Government of Canada, and the province of Nova Scotia
toward our publishing program.

Canada Council   Conseil des Arts
for the Arts   du Canada

July Underwater was drawn in 2014/2015 with support from the Concordia Fine Arts Reading Room. It was originally released as a very small self-published edition. A few small edits have been made for this first widespread printing.

Thank you to all my family, Paige, Andy and Sarah.

This book is dedicated to my friends Sasha and Shayle.

THERE'S ROSEMARY, THAT'S FOR REMEMBRANCE.
PRAY YOU LOVE, REMEMBER

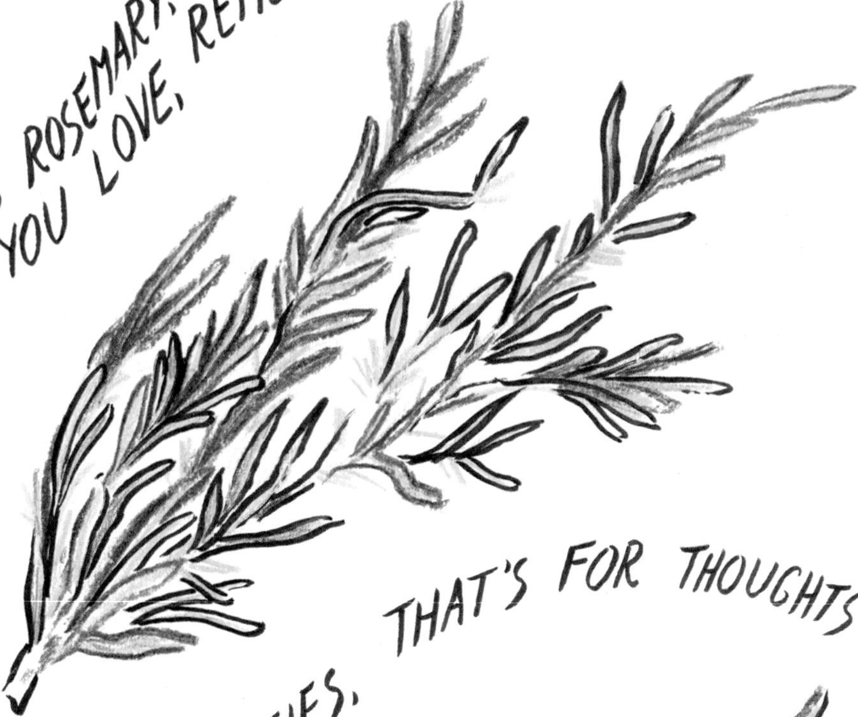

AND THERE IS PANSIES, THAT'S FOR THOUGHTS

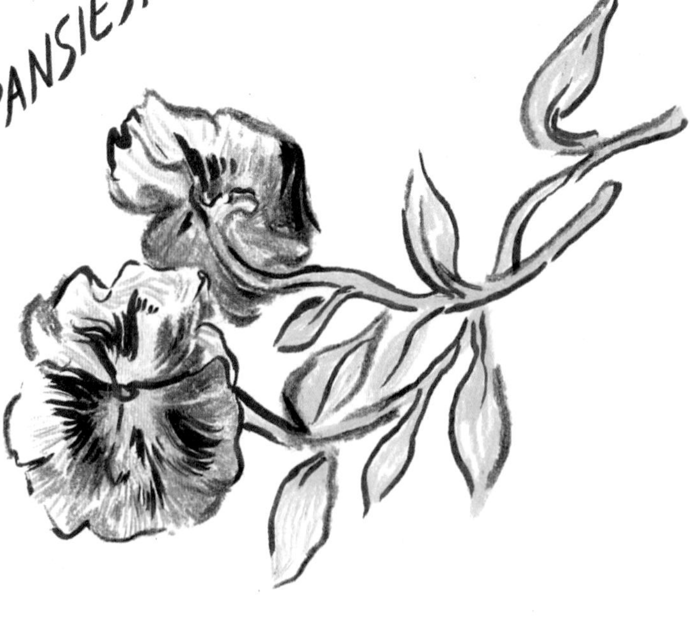

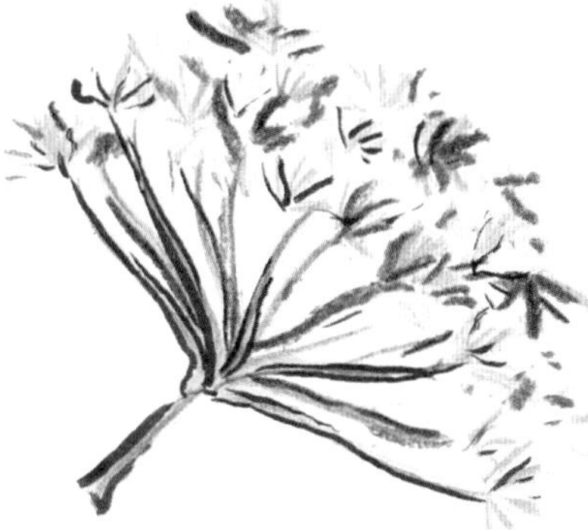

THERE'S FENNEL FOR YOU, AND COLUMBINES

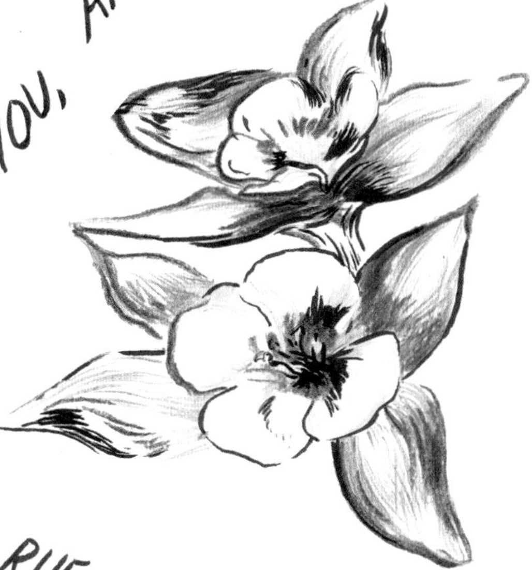

THERE'S RUE FOR YOU, AND
HERE'S SOME FOR ME; WE MAY
CALL IT HERB OF GRACE
O' SUNDAYS. YOU MUST
WEAR YOUR RUE WITH
A DIFFERENCE.

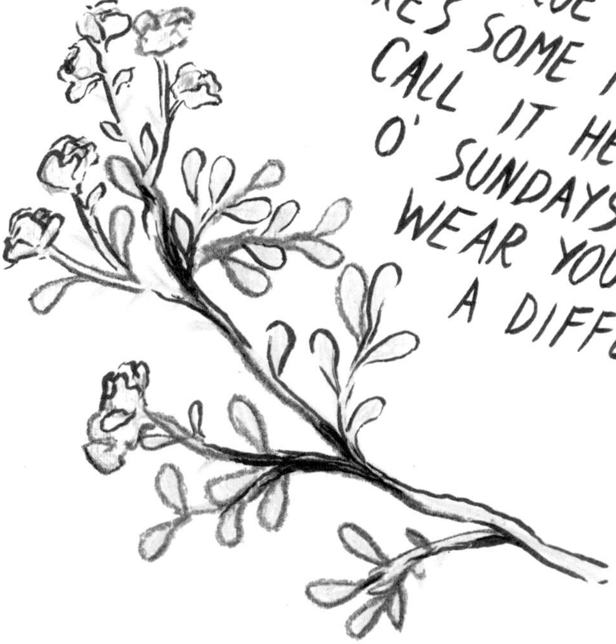

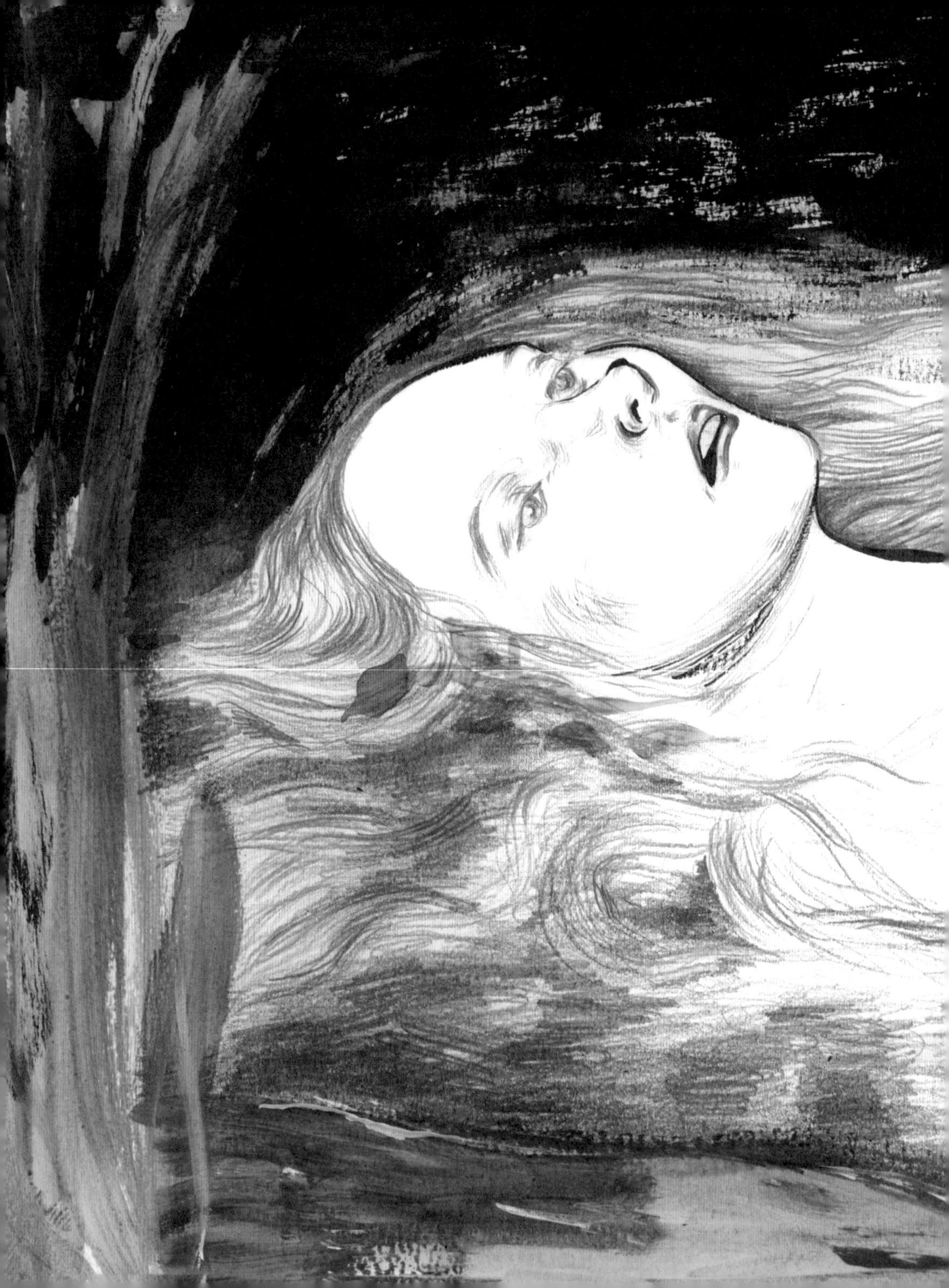

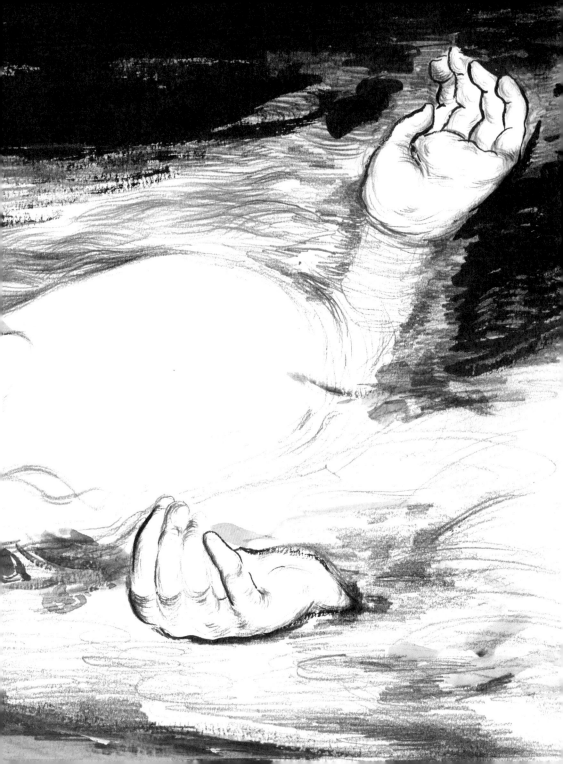

July 15, 2010

Went to Alicia's funeral today. Parents are still out of town so I went on my own and felt kind of awkward.

Afterwards I went to the party on the island with Cara. She's the only person who knew about Alicia which felt weird. Mark was giving me weird vibes. I went swimming and probably got e.coli from Lake Ontario.

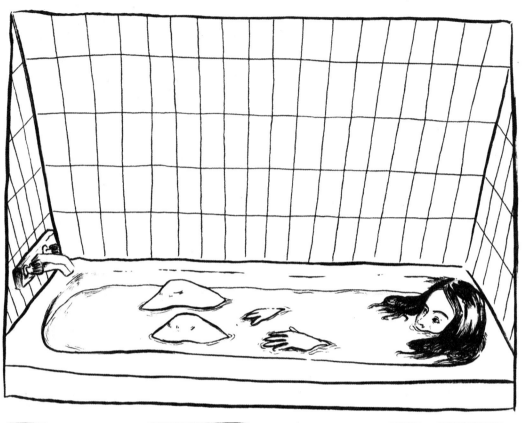

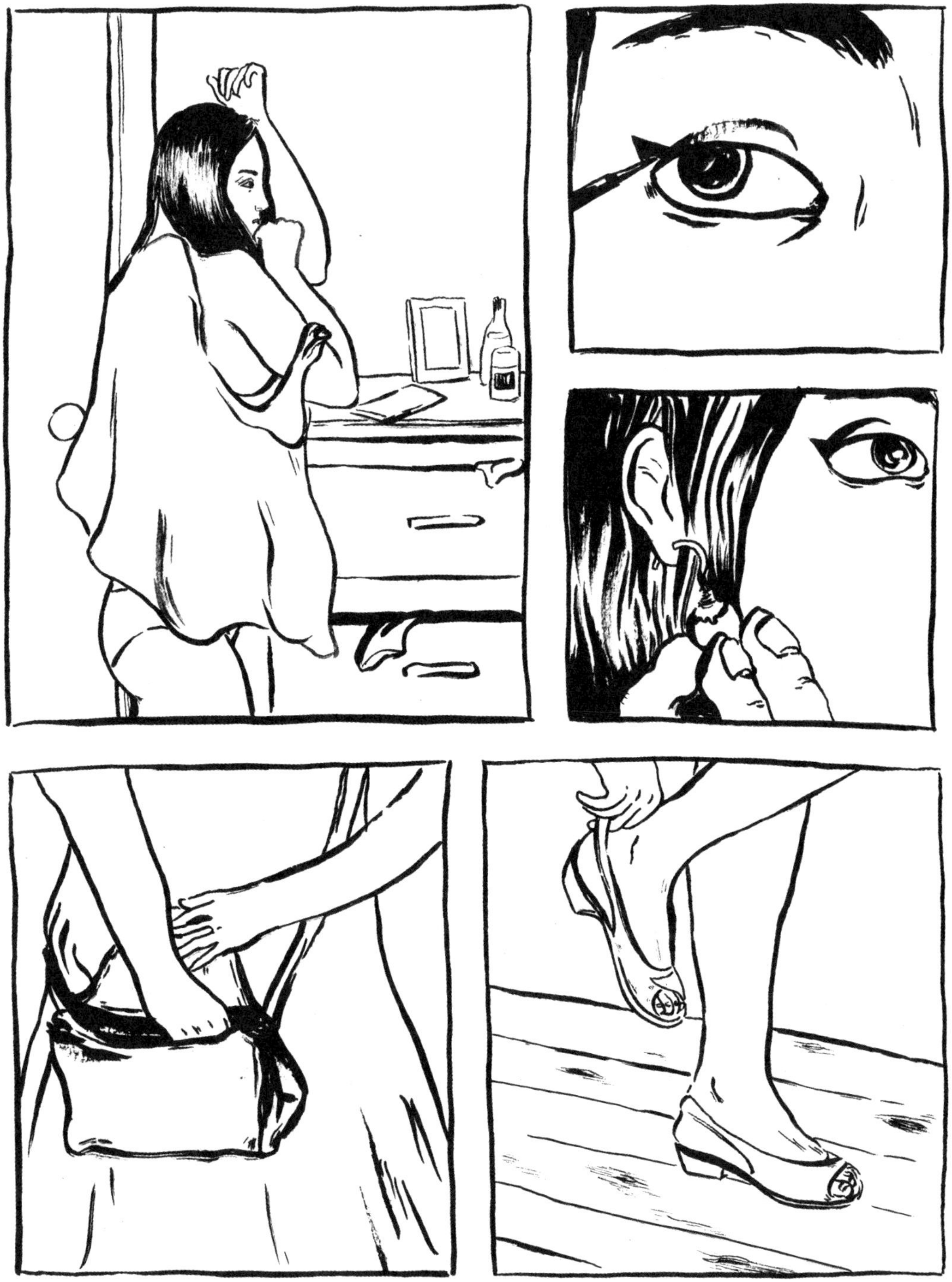

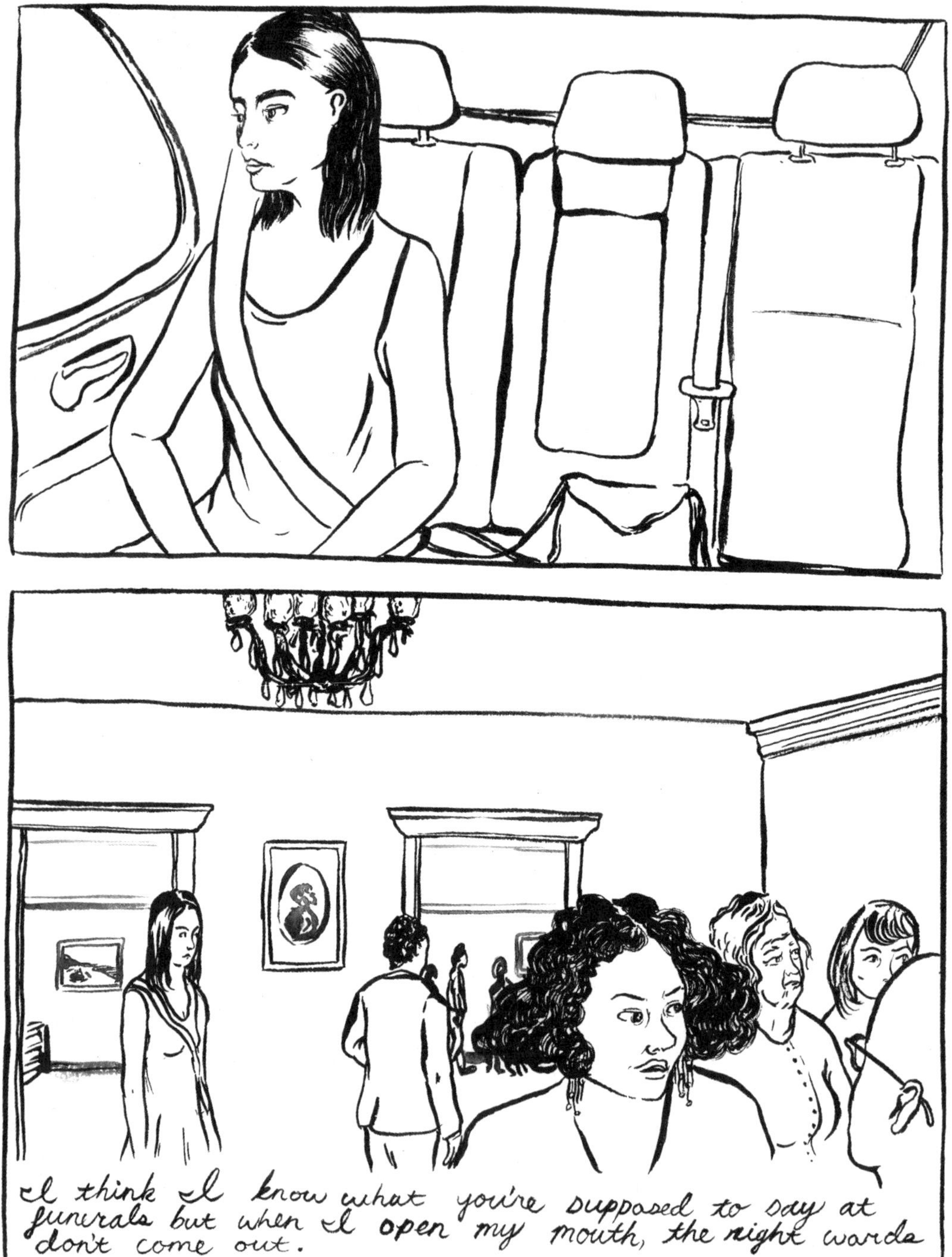
I think I know what you're supposed to say at funerals but when I open my mouth, the right words don't come out.

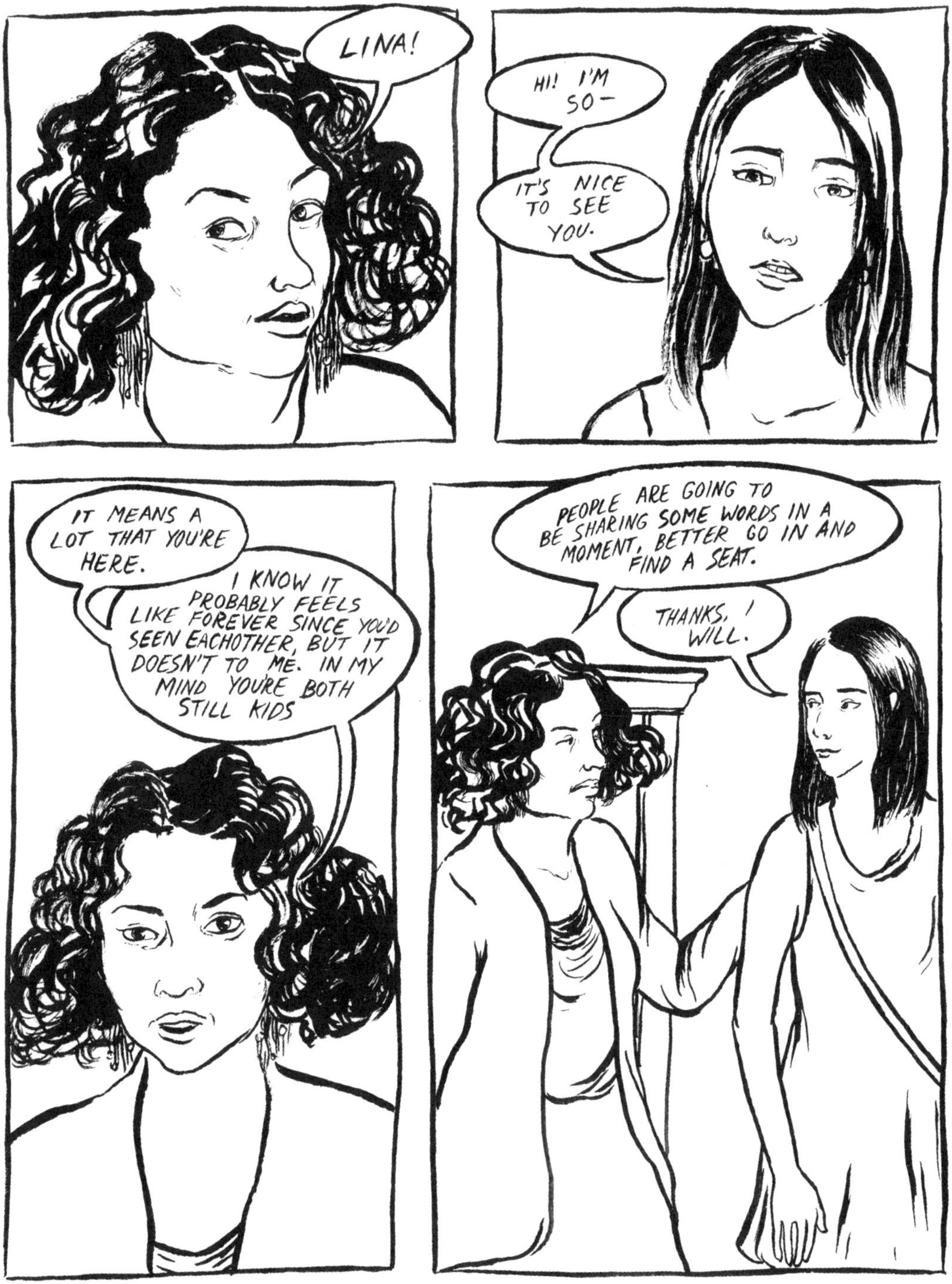
LINA!
HI! I'M SO-
IT'S NICE TO SEE YOU.
IT MEANS A LOT THAT YOU'RE HERE.
I KNOW IT PROBABLY FEELS LIKE FOREVER SINCE YOU'D SEEN EACHOTHER, BUT IT DOESN'T TO ME. IN MY MIND YOU'RE BOTH STILL KIDS
PEOPLE ARE GOING TO BE SHARING SOME WORDS IN A MOMENT, BETTER GO IN AND FIND A SEAT.
THANKS, I WILL.

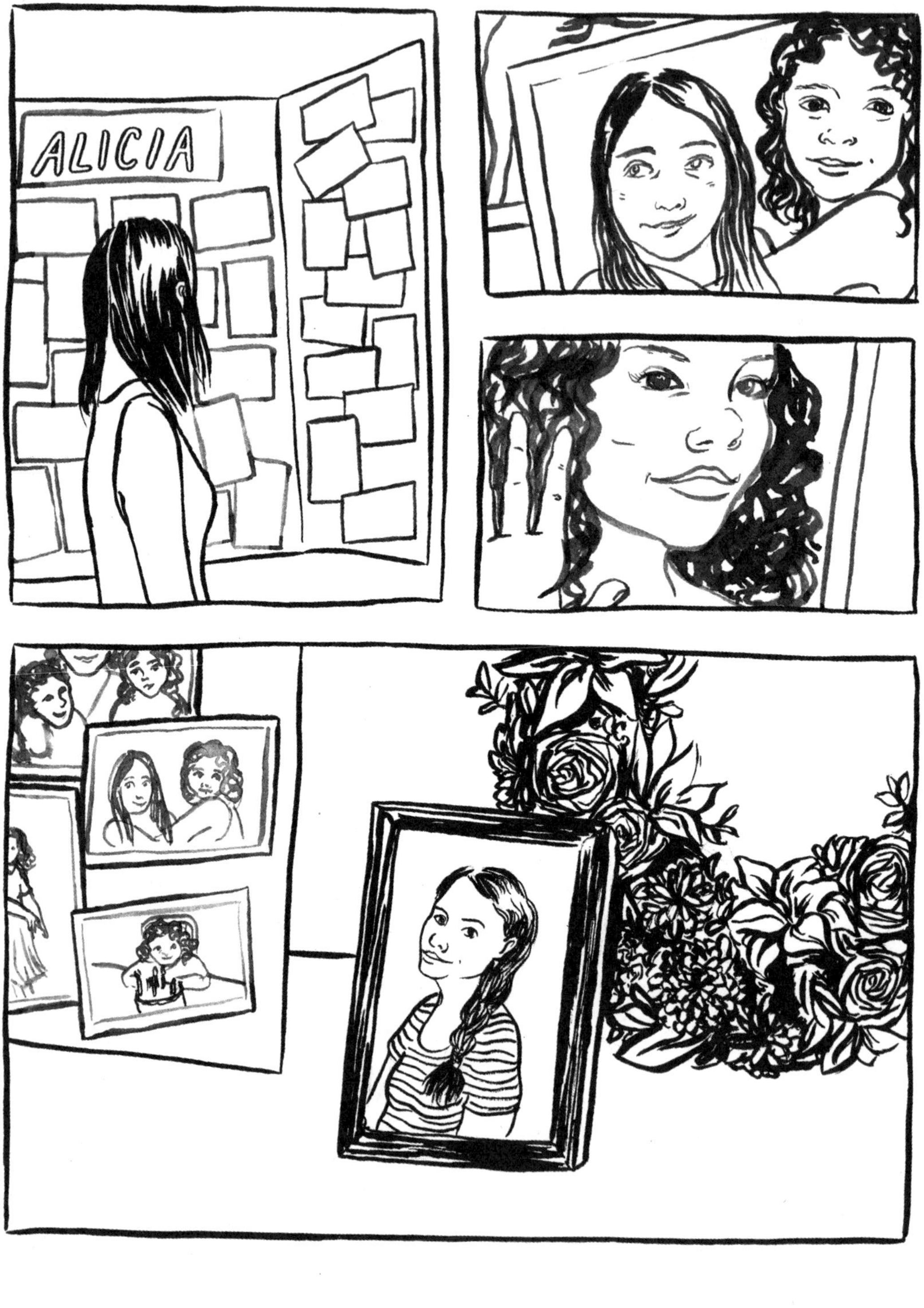
ALICIA

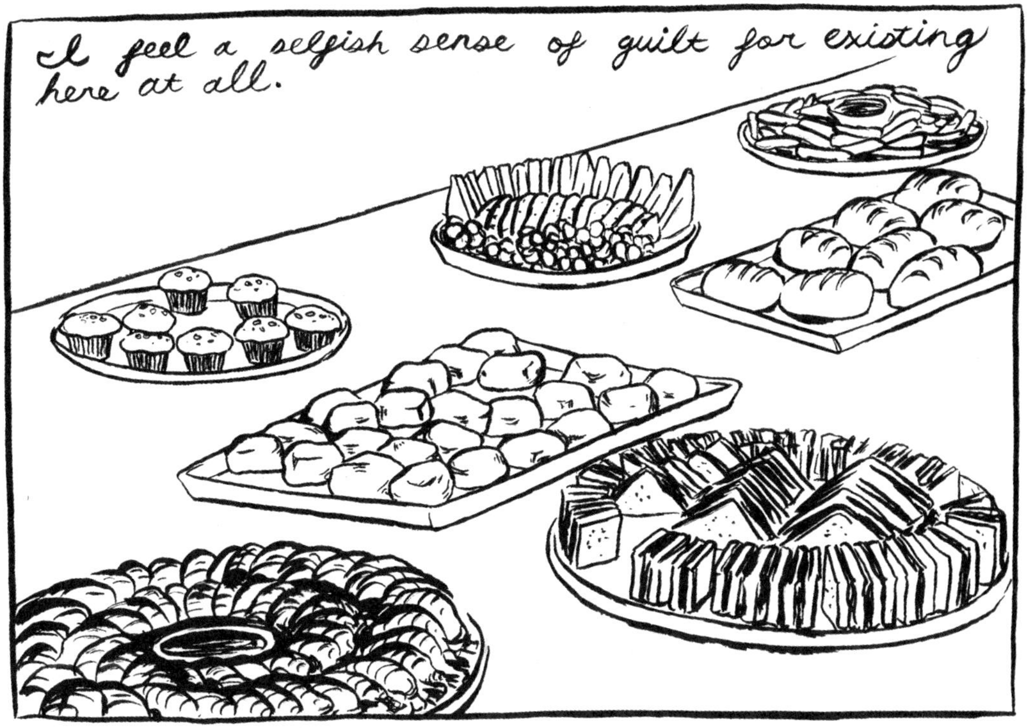
I feel a selfish sense of guilt for existing here at all.

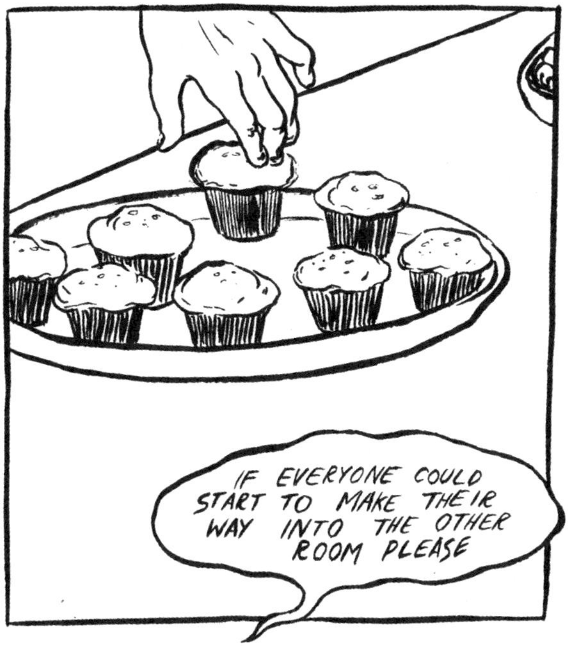
IF EVERYONE COULD START TO MAKE THEIR WAY INTO THE OTHER ROOM PLEASE

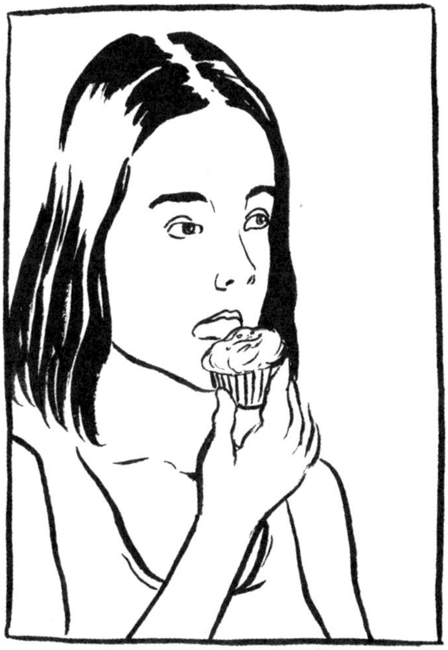

Summer in Toronto is:

-walking barefoot
along the sidewalk after
the sun's gone down,
warm asphalt and softened
tar under your toes

-the buzzing of cicadas
I always associate with
power lines

- so much smog the
air feels sticky

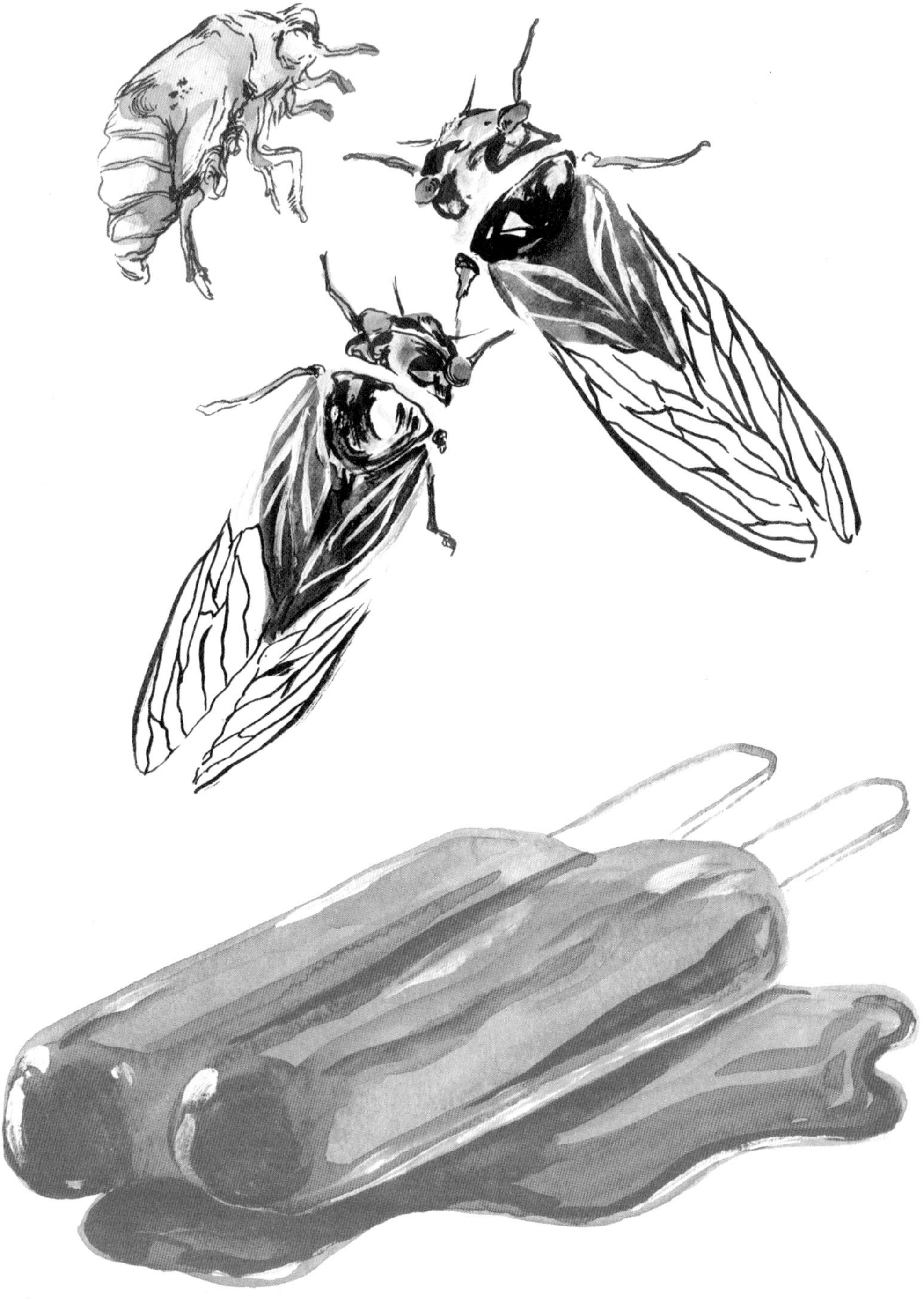

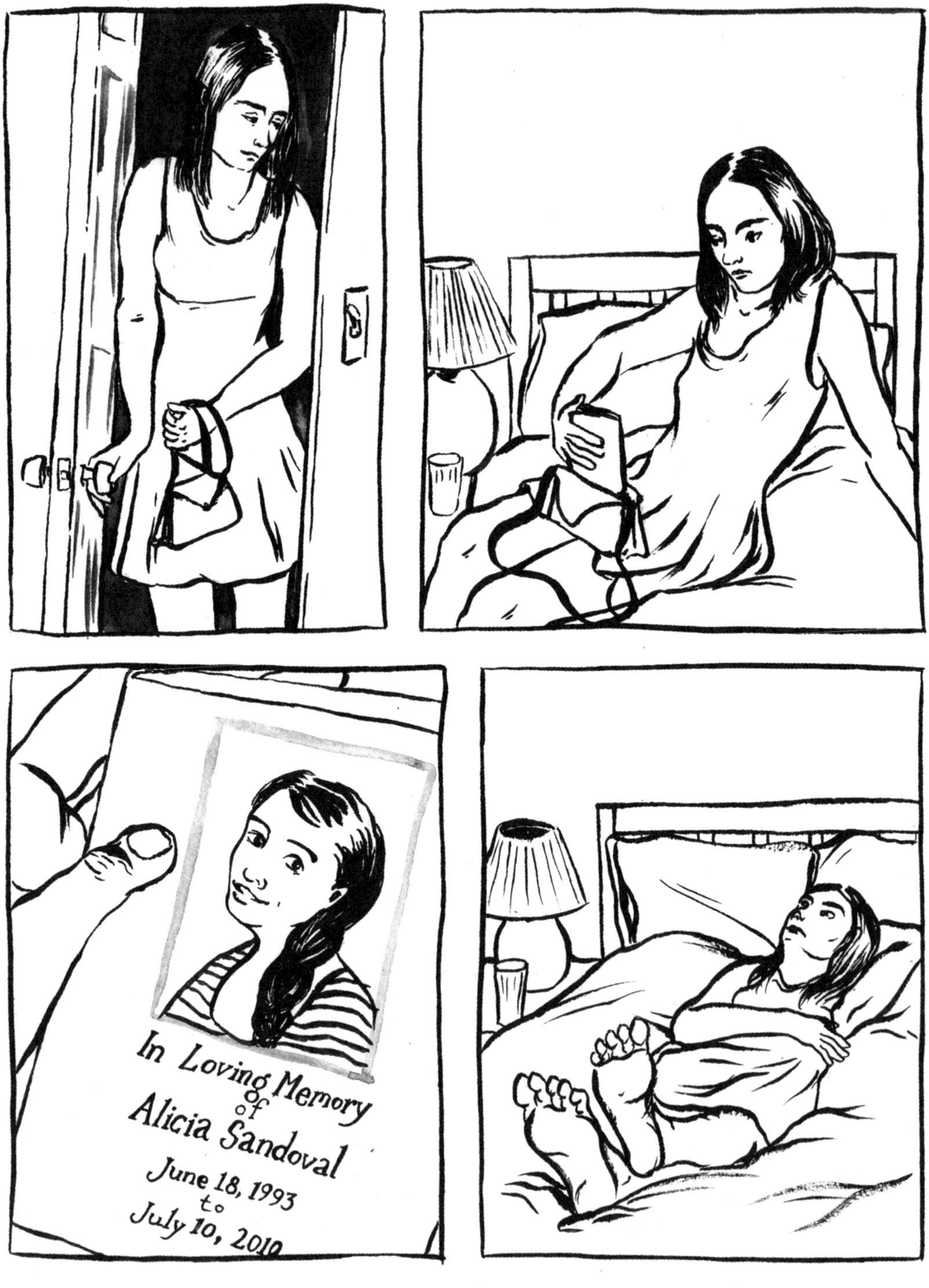
In Loving Memory
of
Alicia Sandoval
June 18, 1993
to
July 10, 2010

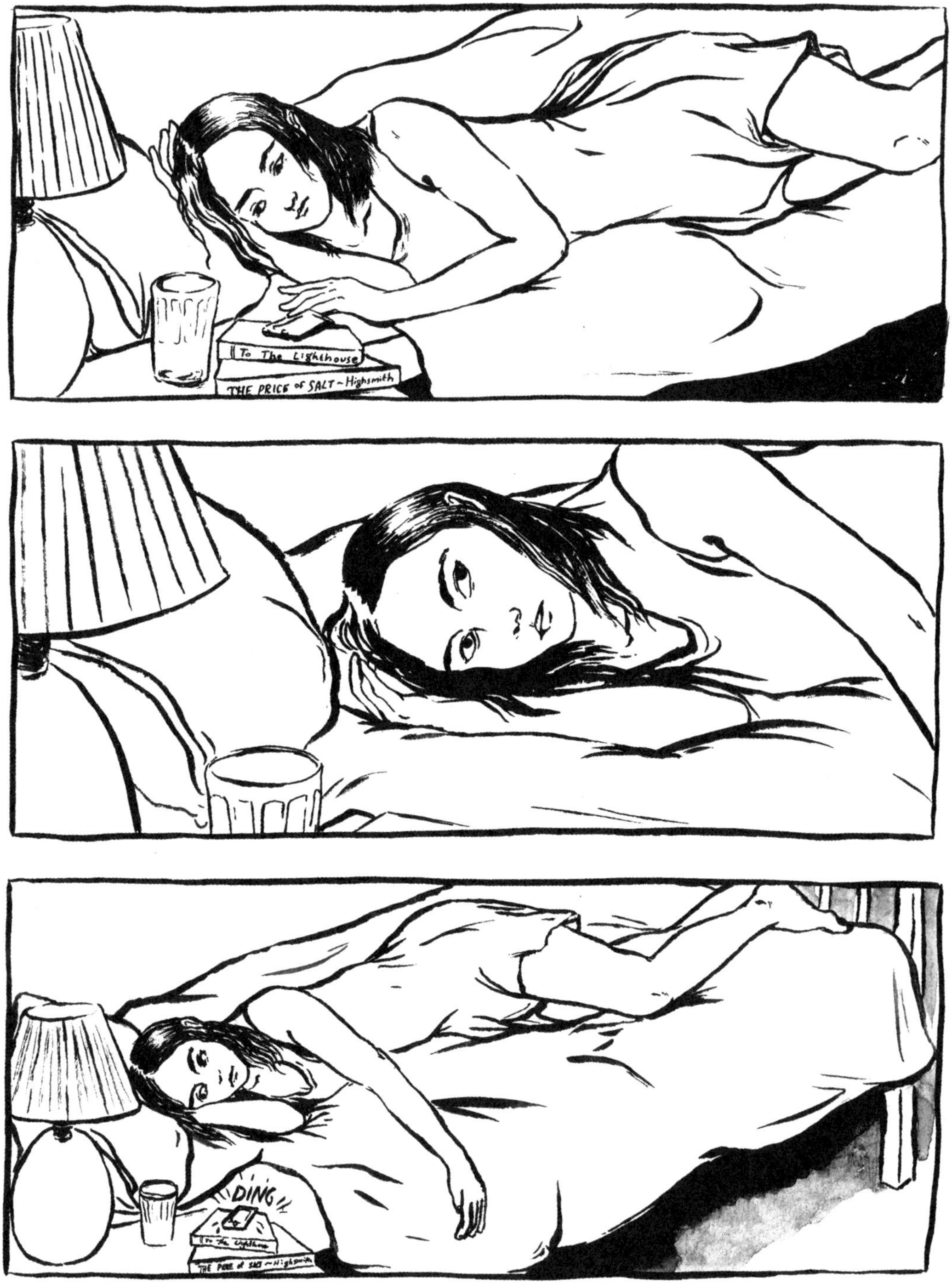
To The Lighthouse
THE PRICE of SALT ~ Highsmith
DING

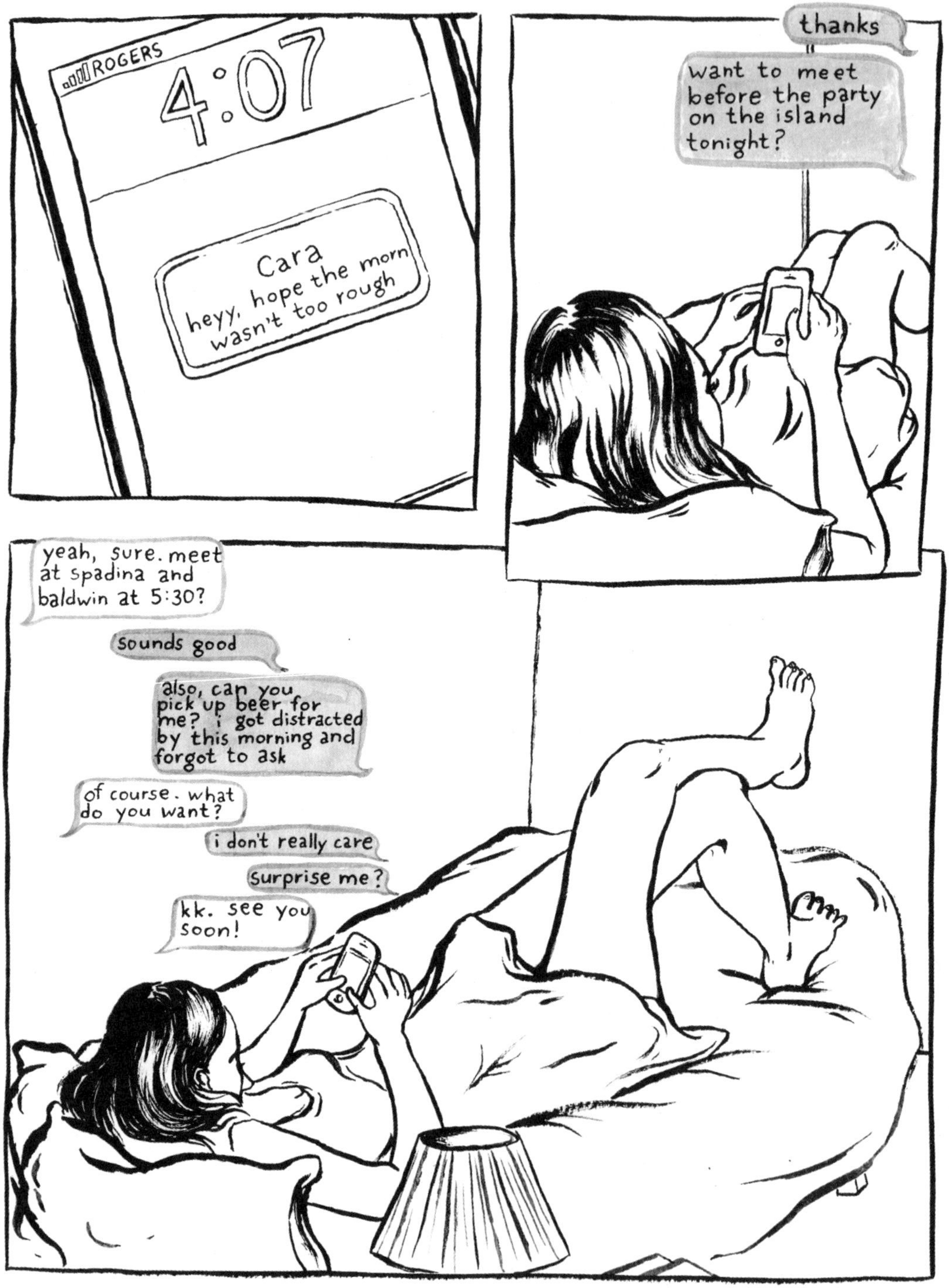
ROGERS
4:07
Cara
heyy, hope the morn wasn't too rough
thanks
want to meet before the party on the island tonight?
yeah, sure. meet at spadina and baldwin at 5:30?
sounds good
also, can you pick up beer for me? i got distracted by this morning and forgot to ask
of course. what do you want?
i don't really care
surprise me?
kk. see you soon!

Things I remember about Alicia:

—running and sliding down the hallway of her house across the street from mine in our sock feet. Playing dress-up and the smell of her closet from the little bags of potpourri in all the drawers.

—her fearlessness around adults, a self assurance I never had.

—hanging around her mom's painting studio in the summer when school was out

—that day on the island at dusk

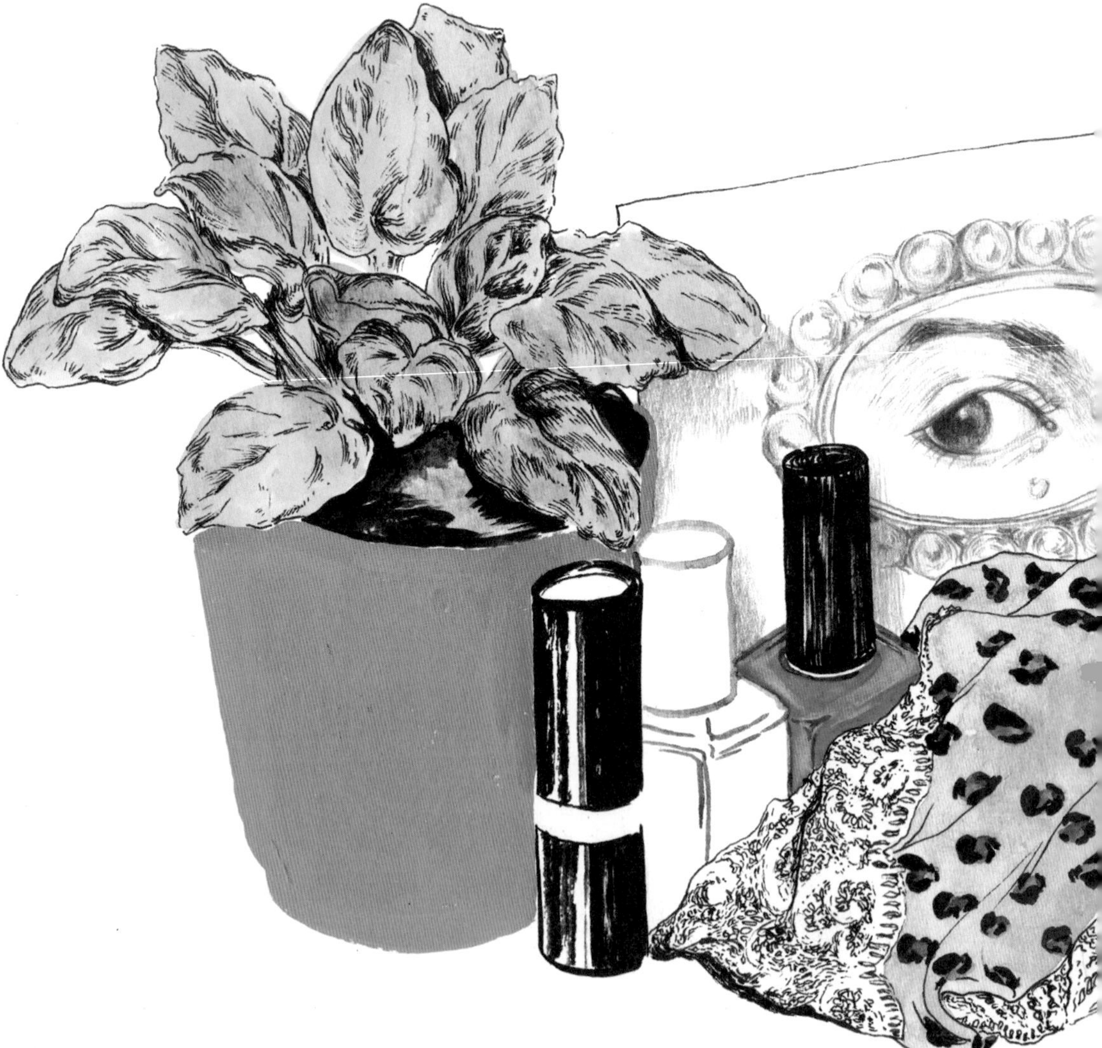

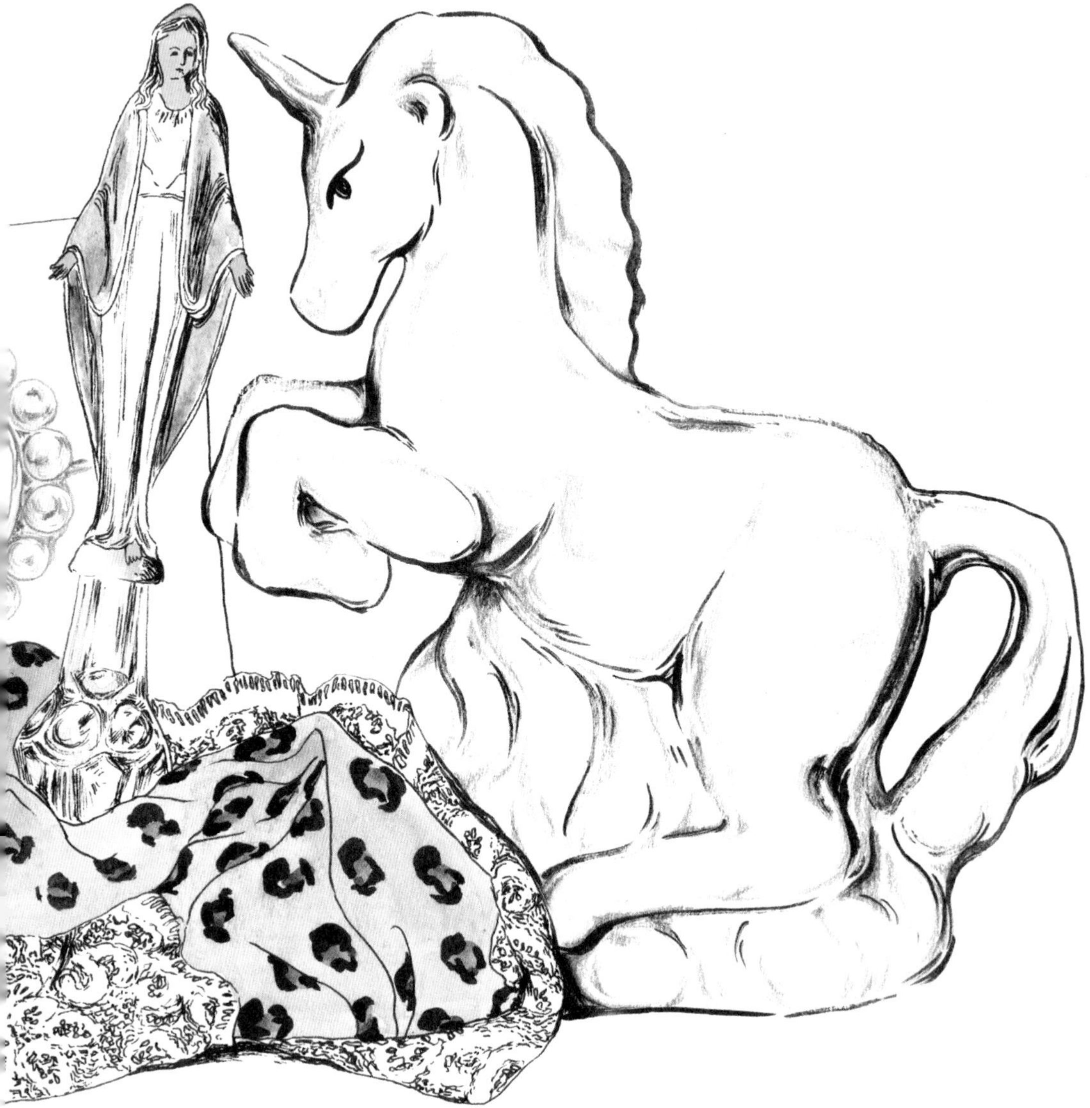

I read so much this week.

first I finished To The Lighthouse. Mirta is my favourite in it — the part where she talks about the feeling of The Glow.

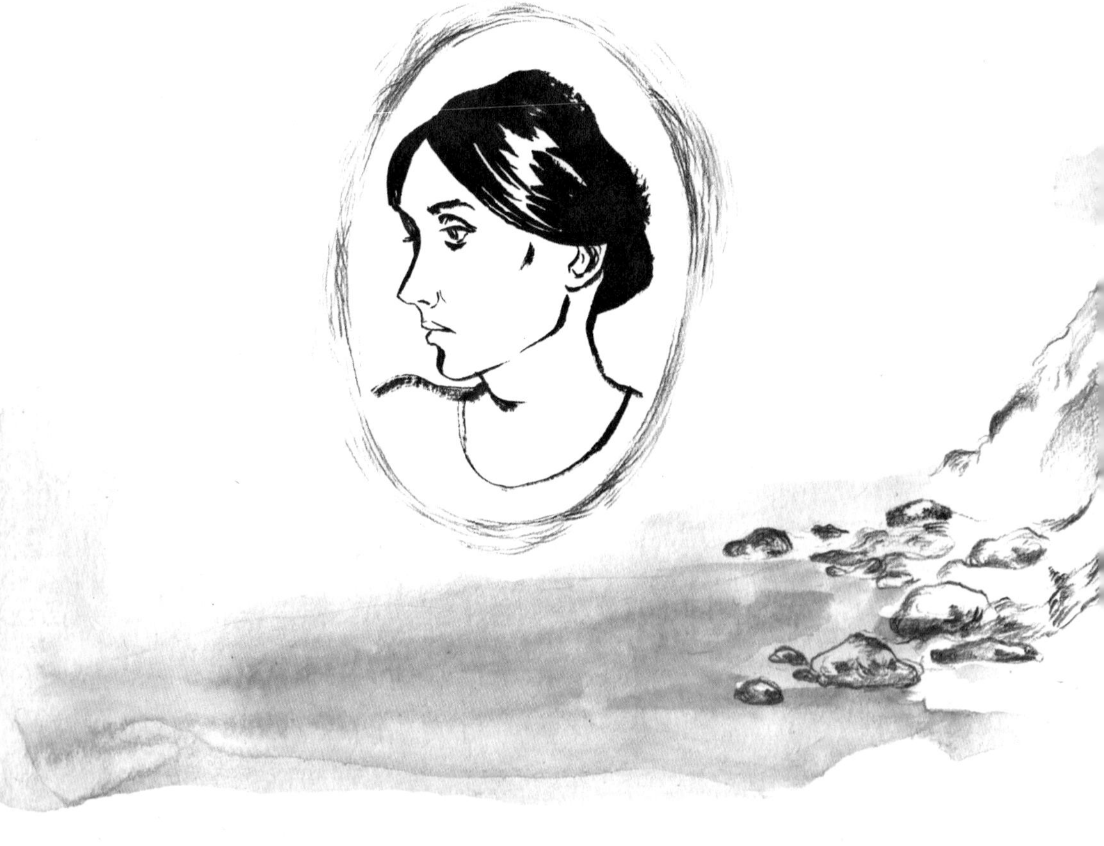

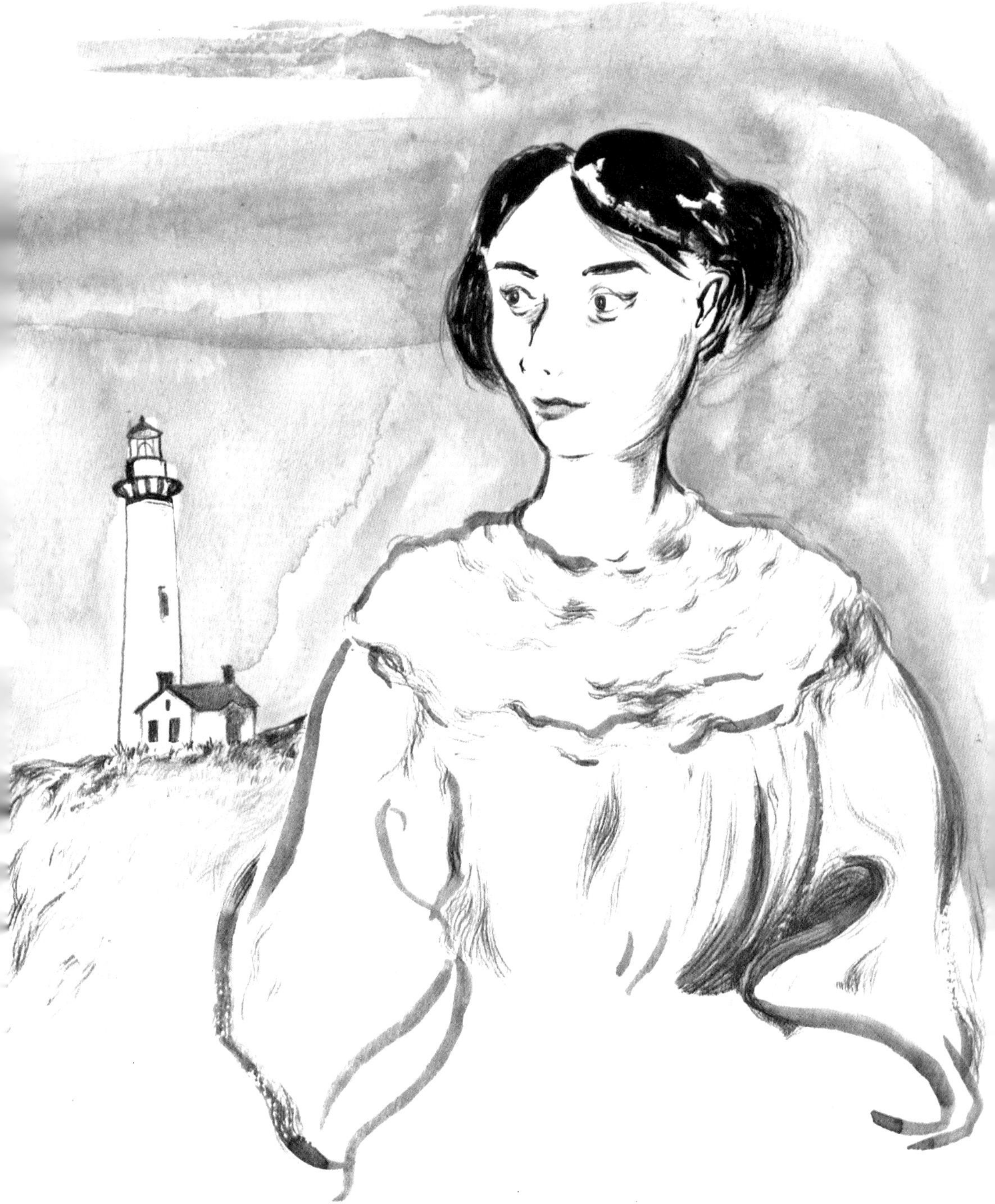

Last night I was reading parts of The Price of Salt again. Its supposed to be a kind of proto-Lolita that inspired Nabokov to write his book but it's also so Thelma + Louise.

It's about this girl Therese who meets this woman Carol and falls in love, and then they run off and drive across America.

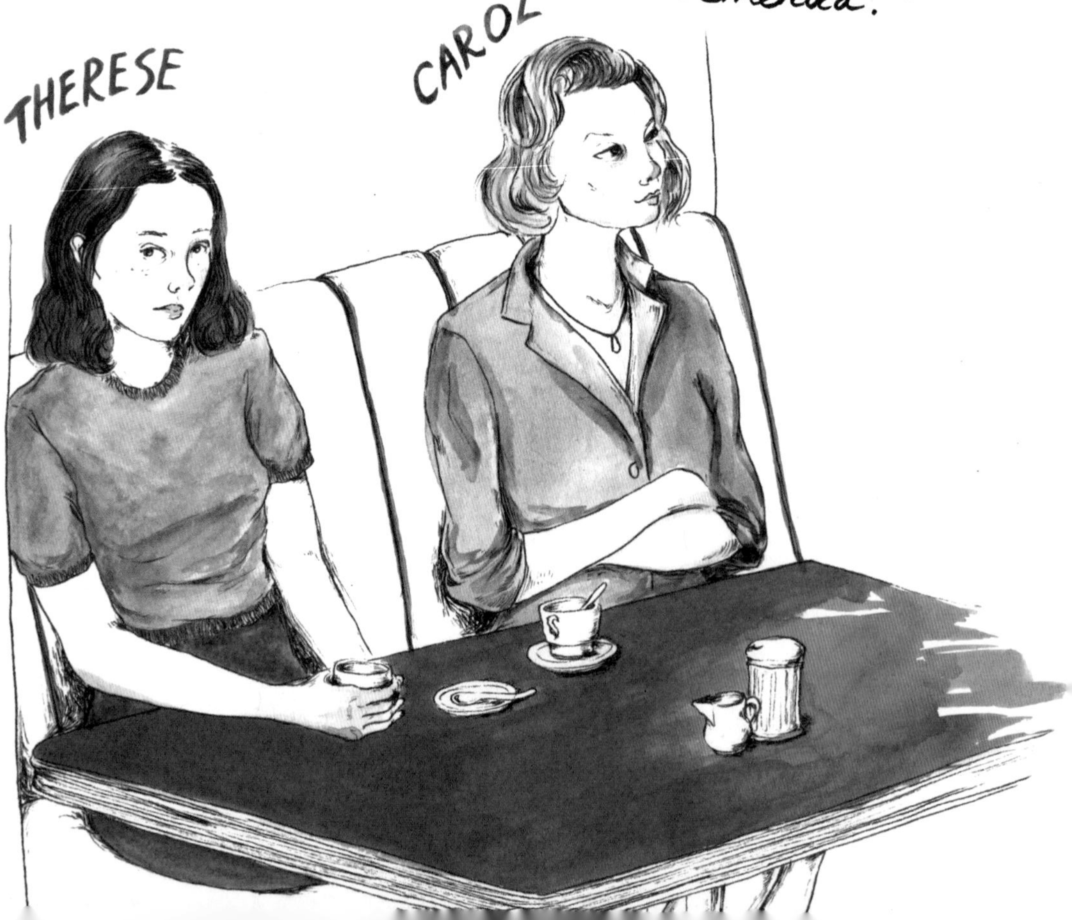
THERESE
CAROL

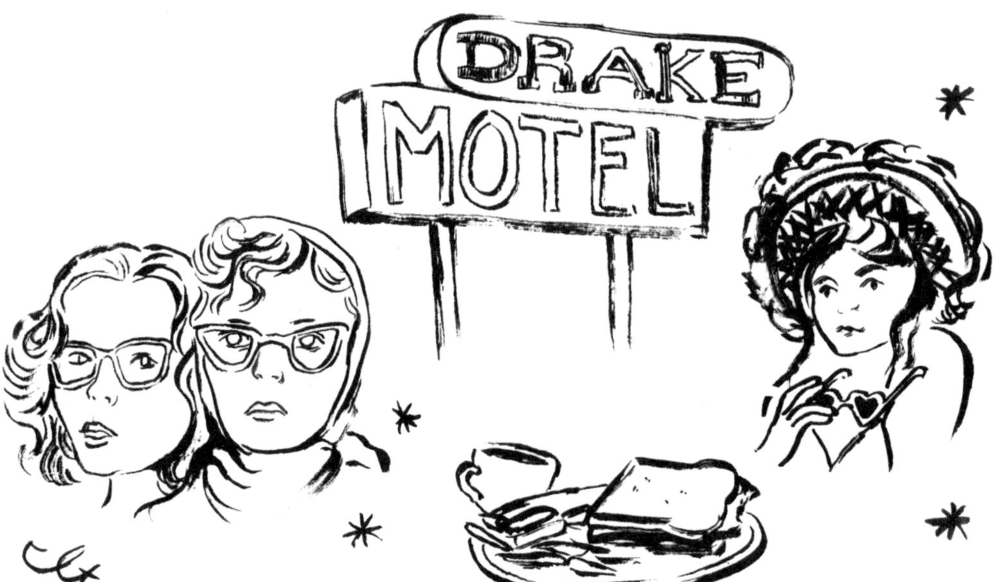
DRAKE
MOTEL

It was written by Patricia Highsmith in 1952 and published as a pulp novel, one of the first books that didn't end in tragedy for its queer protagonists.

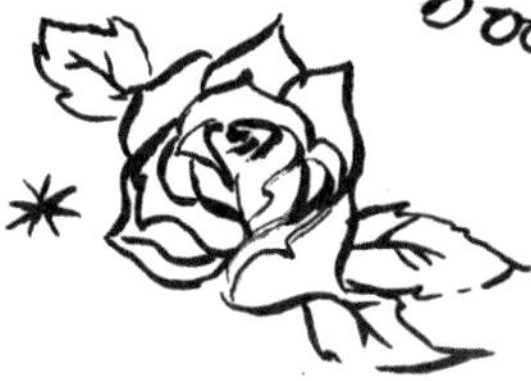

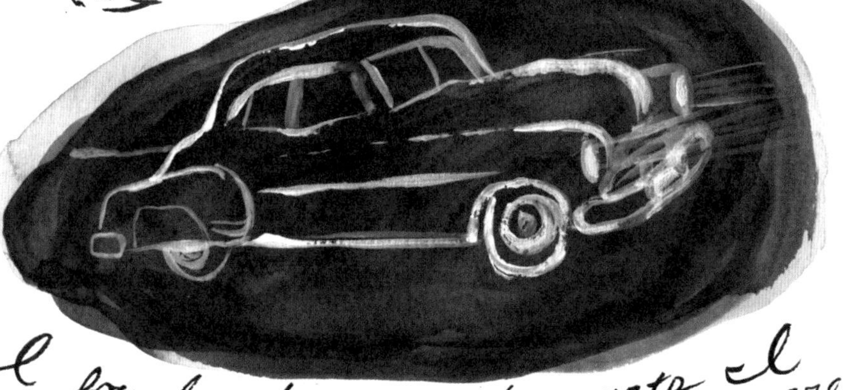

I found that all the parts I remembered the most vividly were much less important than I'd thought.

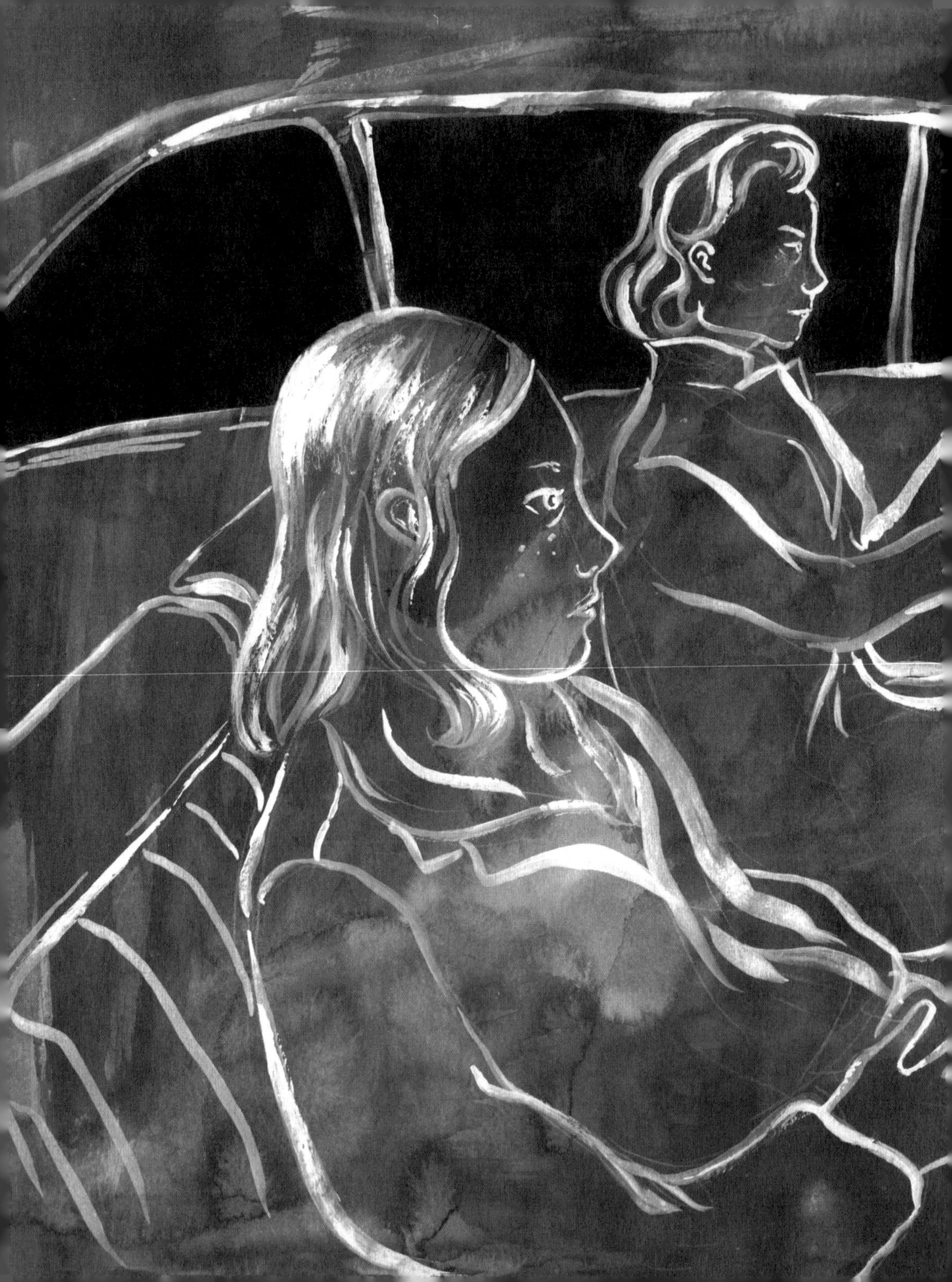

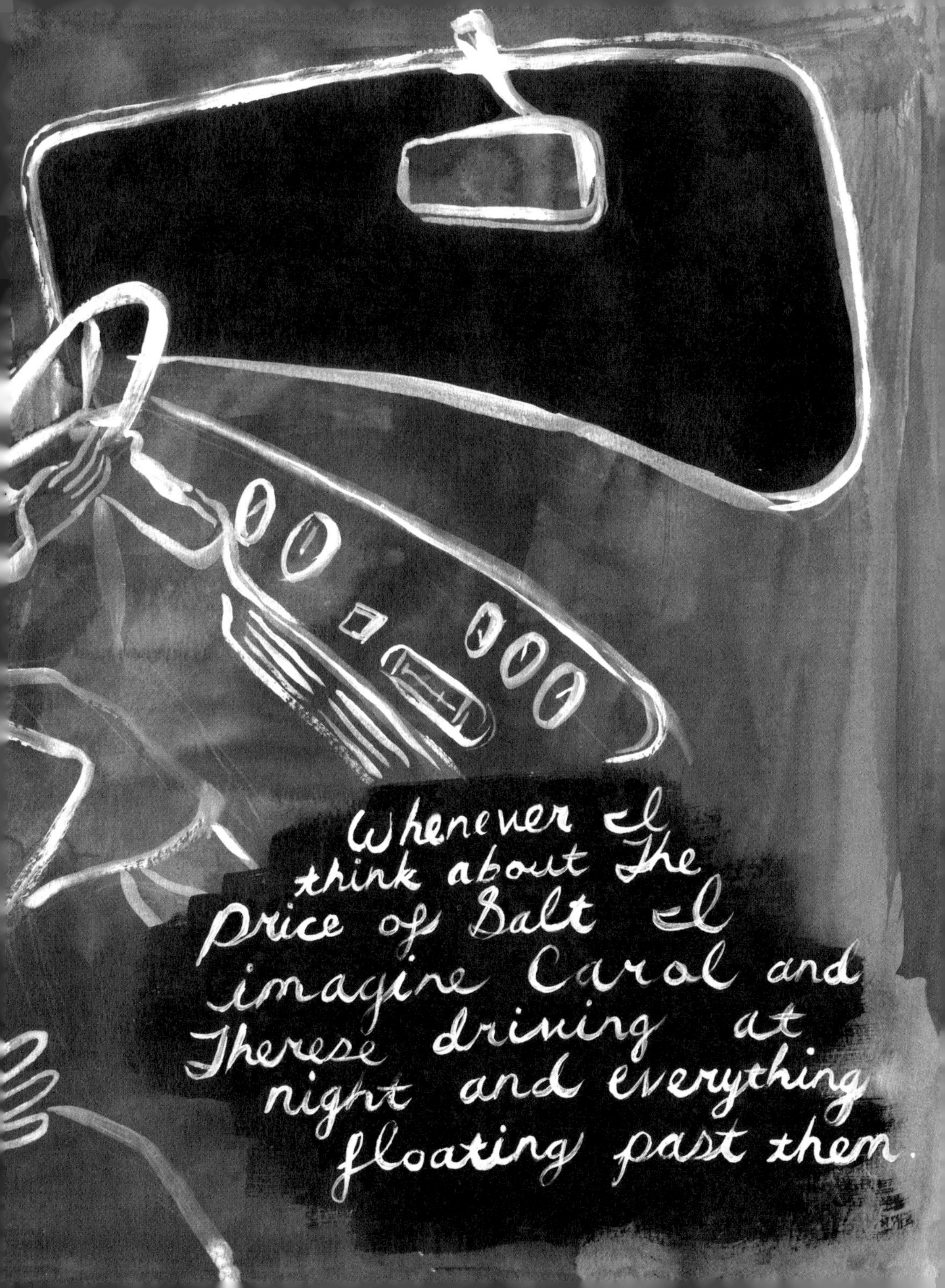
Whenever I
think about The
Price of Salt I
imagine Carol and
Therese driving at
night and everything
floating past them.

In Patricia Highsmith's story, when Therese cuts ties with her life in New York she finds herself in a void, and in doing so seems to become a void herself.
WHAT A STRANGE GIRL YOU ARE.
FLUNG OUT OF SPACE.
Carol says to Therese.

flung out of
space is how
I feel this summer.
flung out of space is the
feeling of a long drive
in the back seat of a
car, the feeling of a
lake at night.

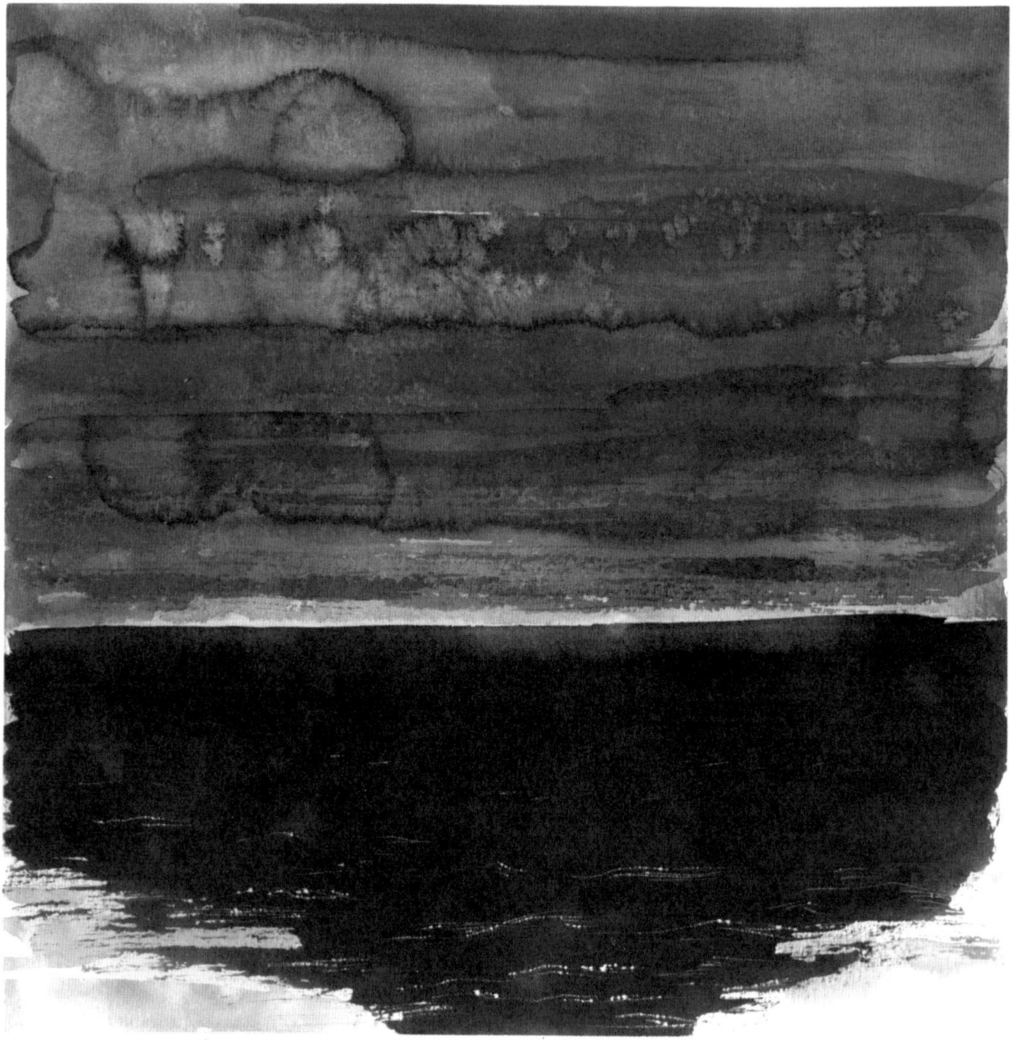

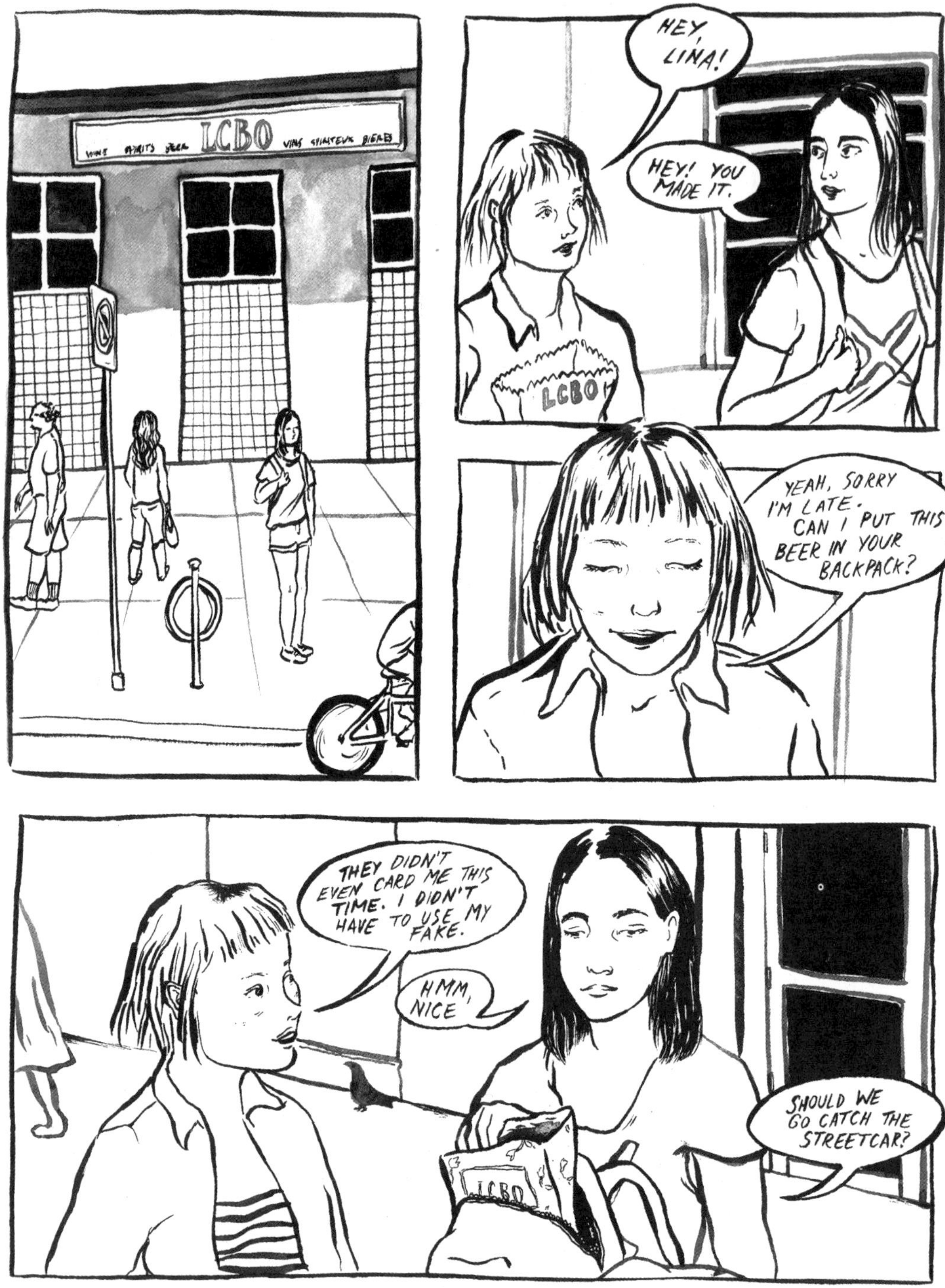
LCBO
WINE SPIRITS BEER
VINS SPIRITUEUX BIERES
HEY, LINA!
HEY! YOU MADE IT.
LCBO
YEAH, SORRY I'M LATE. CAN I PUT THIS BEER IN YOUR BACKPACK?
THEY DIDN'T EVEN CARD ME THIS TIME. I DIDN'T HAVE TO USE MY FAKE.
HMM, NICE
LCBO
SHOULD WE GO CATCH THE STREETCAR?

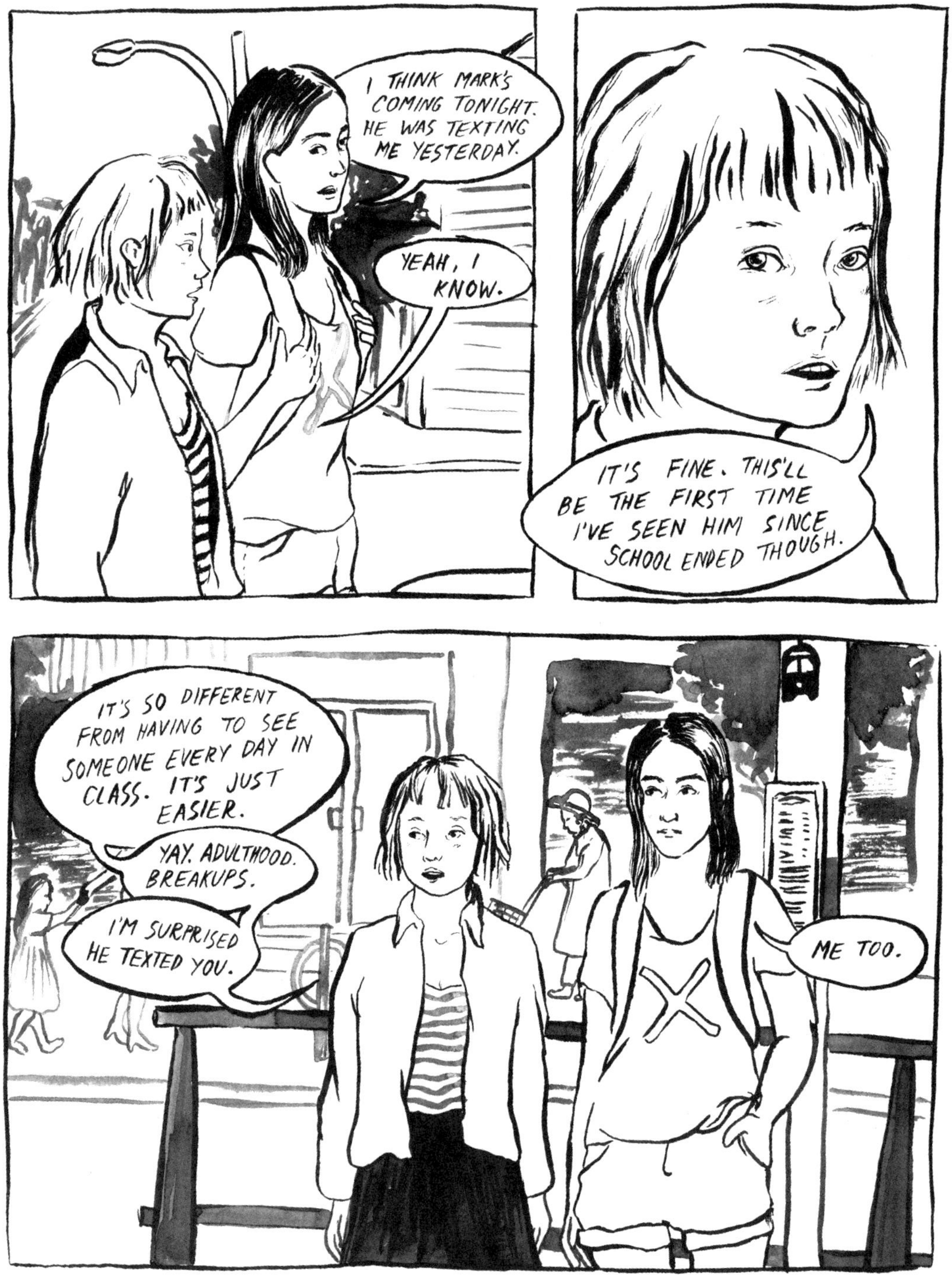
I THINK MARK'S COMING TONIGHT. HE WAS TEXTING ME YESTERDAY.
YEAH, I KNOW.
IT'S FINE. THIS'LL BE THE FIRST TIME I'VE SEEN HIM SINCE SCHOOL ENDED THOUGH.
IT'S SO DIFFERENT FROM HAVING TO SEE SOMEONE EVERY DAY IN CLASS. IT'S JUST EASIER.
YAY. ADULTHOOD. BREAKUPS.
I'M SURPRISED HE TEXTED YOU.
ME TOO.

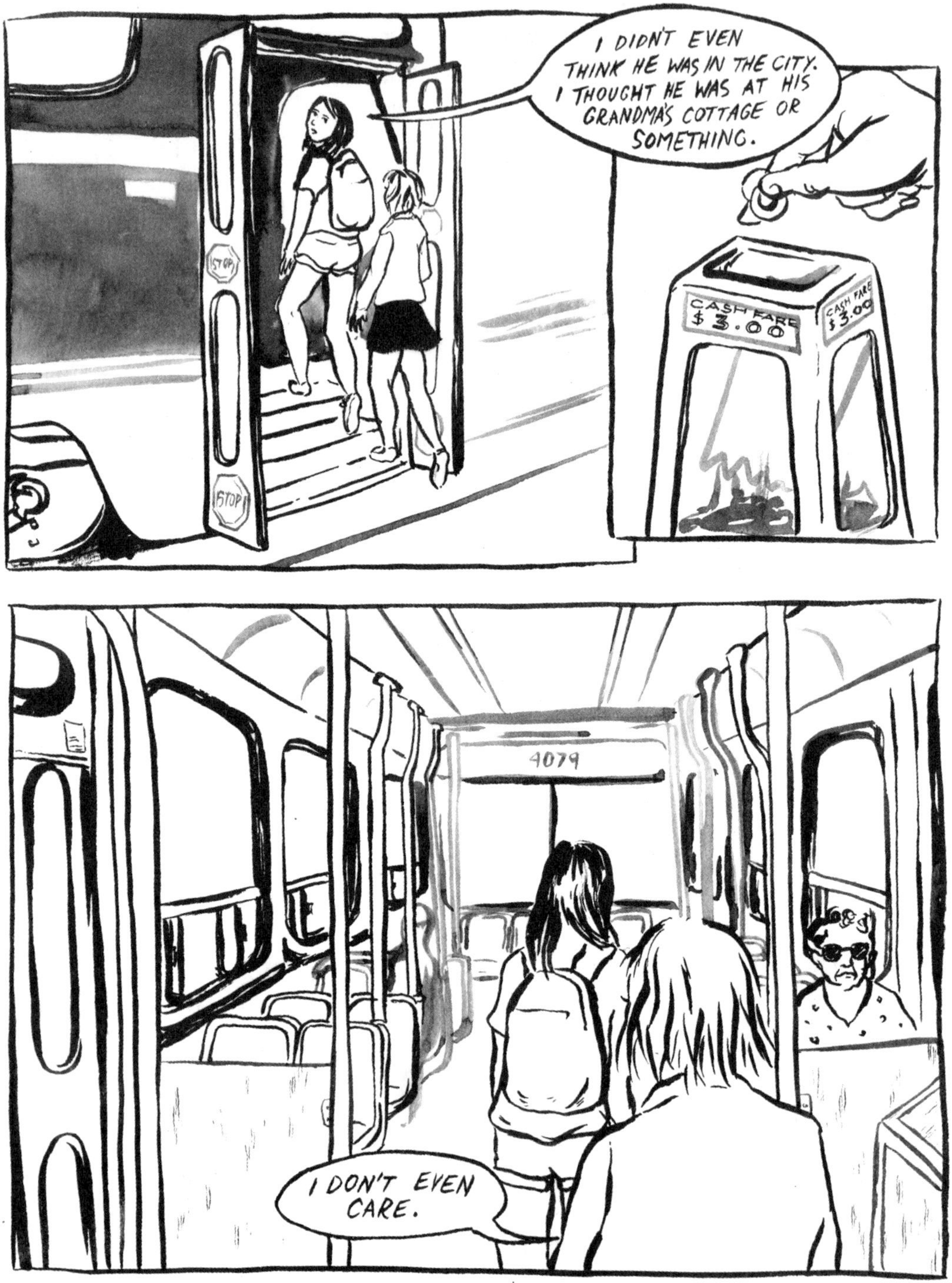
I DIDN'T EVEN THINK HE WAS IN THE CITY. I THOUGHT HE WAS AT HIS GRANDMA'S COTTAGE OR SOMETHING.
STOP
STOP
CASH FARE $3.00
CASH FARE $3.00
4079
I DON'T EVEN CARE.

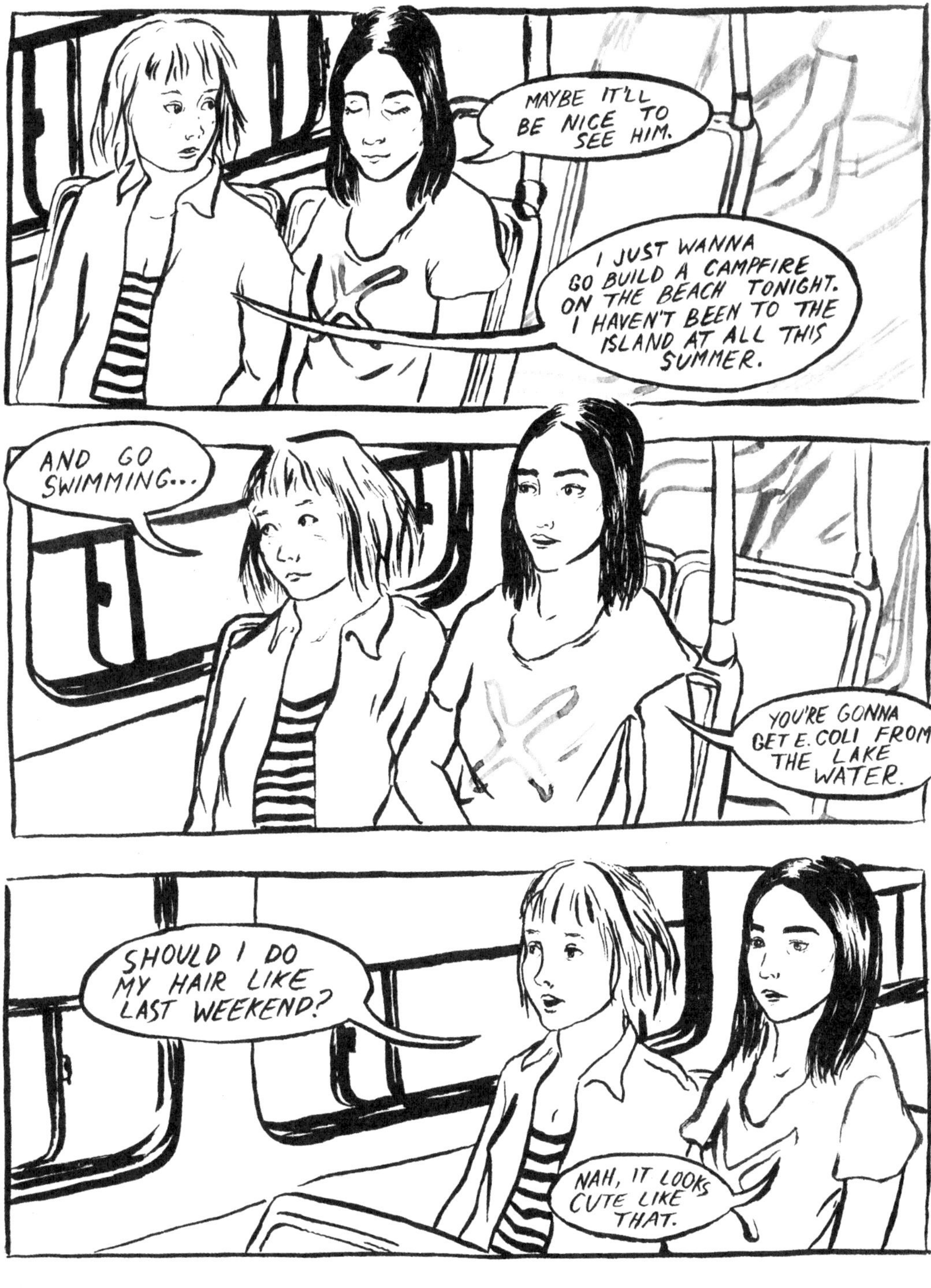
MAYBE IT'LL BE NICE TO SEE HIM.
I JUST WANNA GO BUILD A CAMPFIRE ON THE BEACH TONIGHT. I HAVEN'T BEEN TO THE ISLAND AT ALL THIS SUMMER.
AND GO SWIMMING...
YOU'RE GONNA GET E. COLI FROM THE LAKE WATER.
SHOULD I DO MY HAIR LIKE LAST WEEKEND?
NAH, IT LOOKS CUTE LIKE THAT.

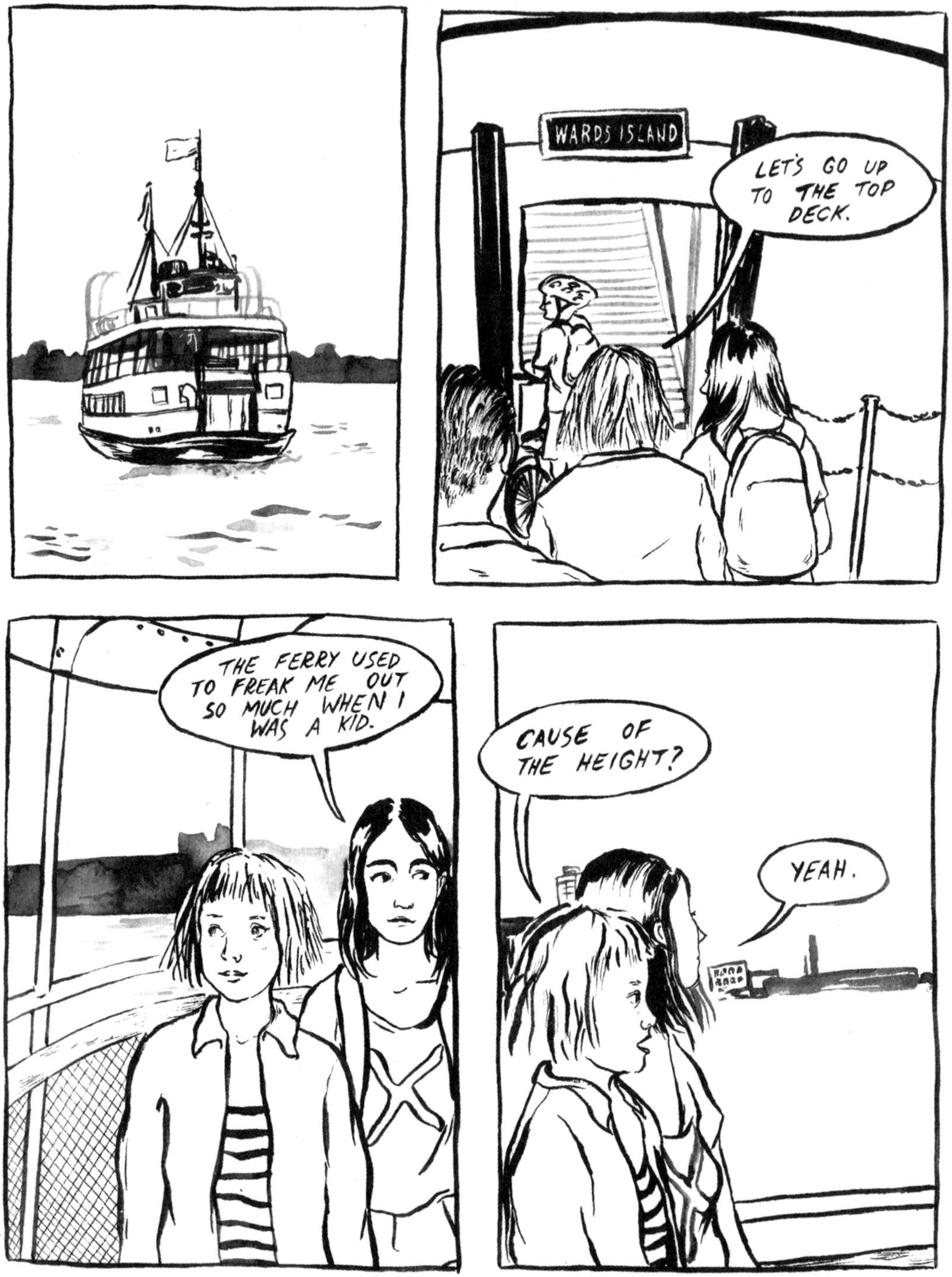
WARDS ISLAND
LET'S GO UP TO THE TOP DECK.
THE FERRY USED TO FREAK ME OUT SO MUCH WHEN I WAS A KID.
CAUSE OF THE HEIGHT?
YEAH.

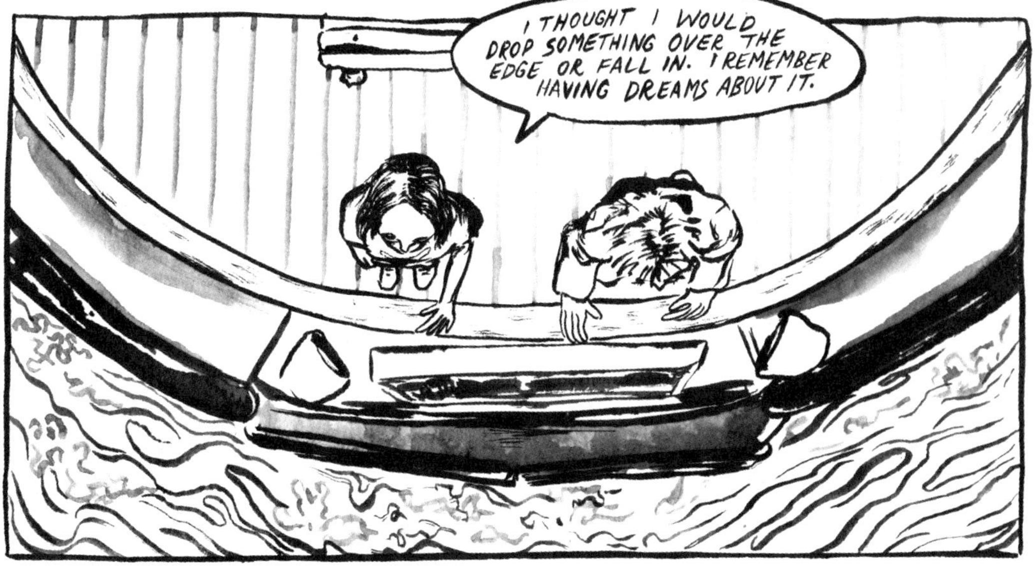
I THOUGHT I WOULD DROP SOMETHING OVER THE EDGE OR FALL IN. I REMEMBER HAVING DREAMS ABOUT IT.

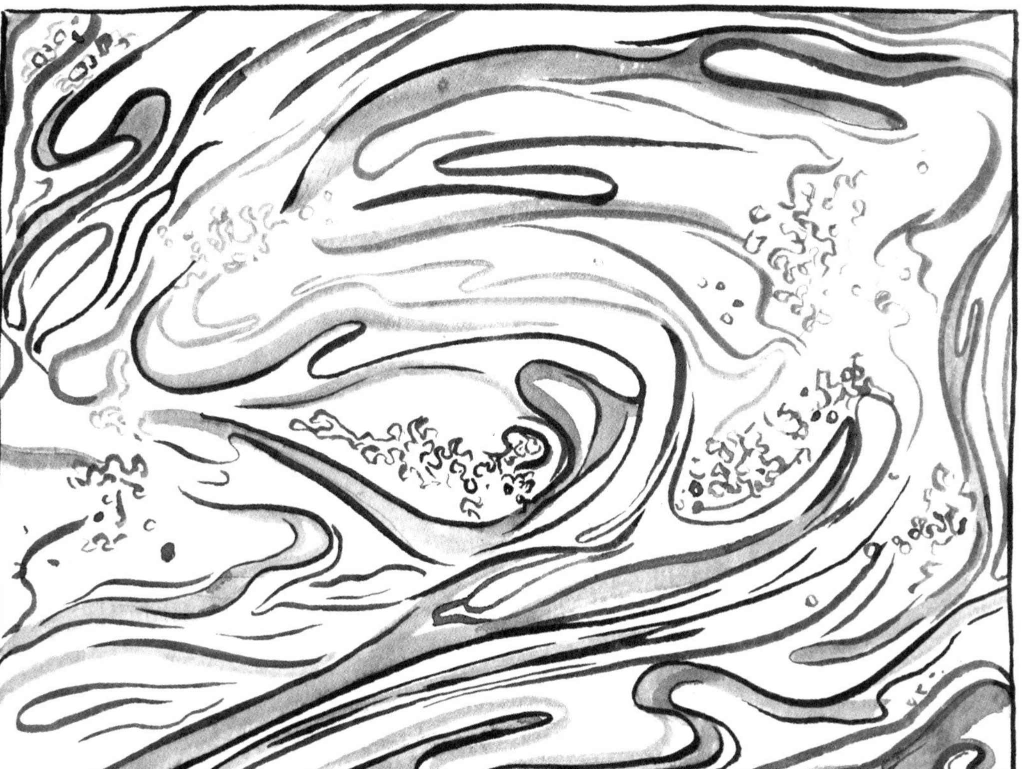

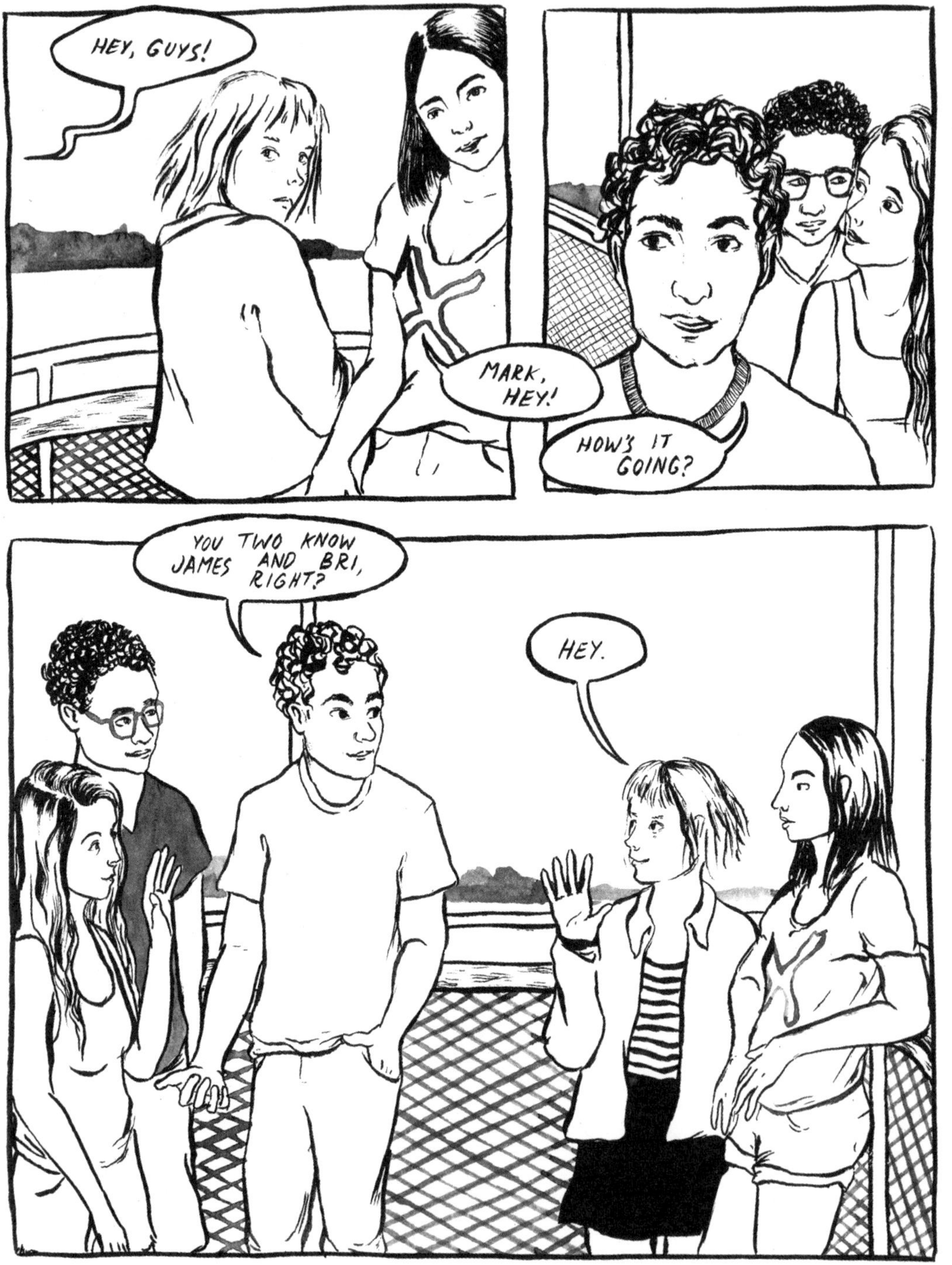
HEY, GUYS!
MARK, HEY!
HOW'S IT GOING?
YOU TWO KNOW JAMES AND BRI, RIGHT?
HEY.

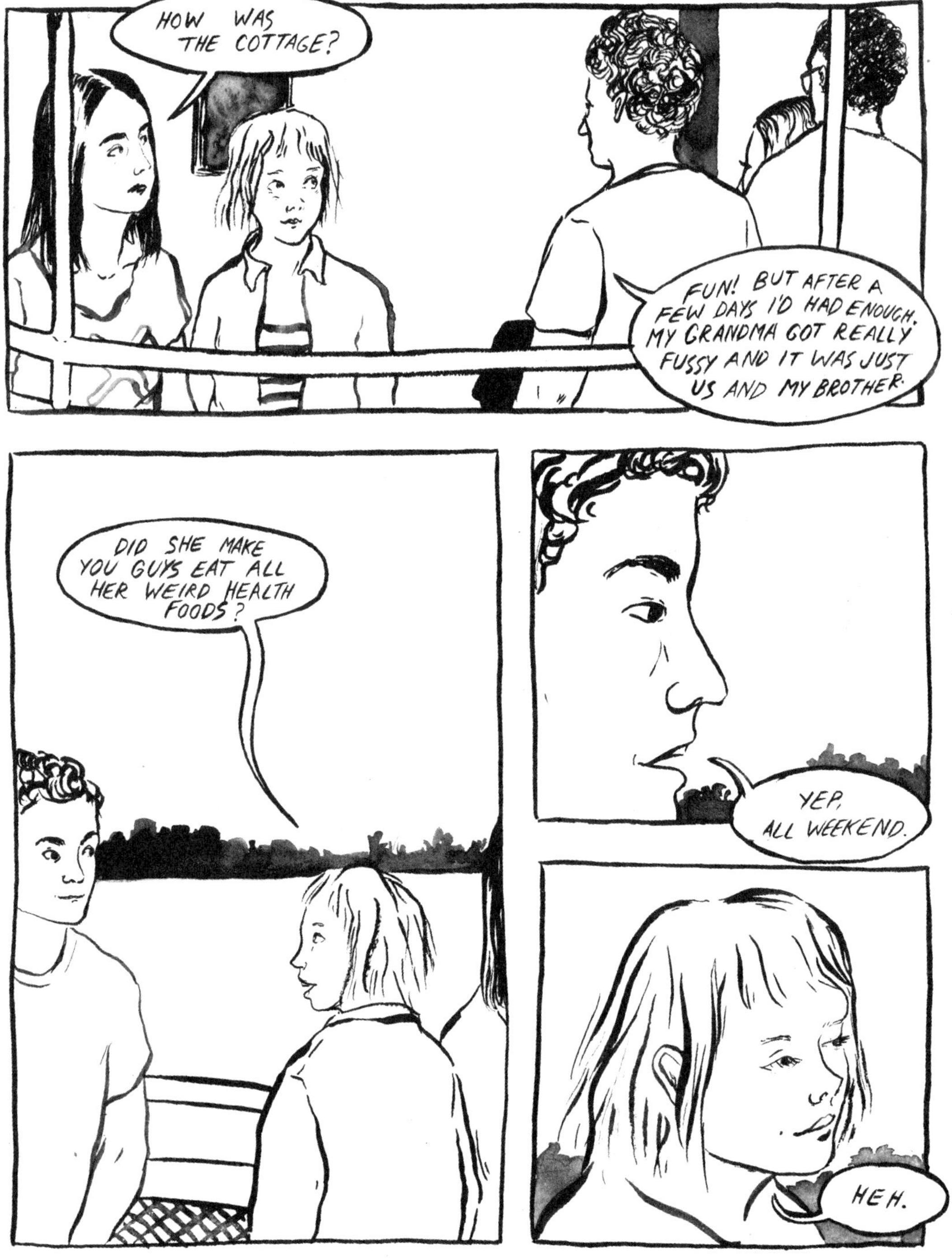
HOW WAS THE COTTAGE?
FUN! BUT AFTER A FEW DAYS I'D HAD ENOUGH. MY GRANDMA GOT REALLY FUSSY AND IT WAS JUST US AND MY BROTHER.
DID SHE MAKE YOU GUYS EAT ALL HER WEIRD HEALTH FOODS?
YEP, ALL WEEKEND.
HEH.

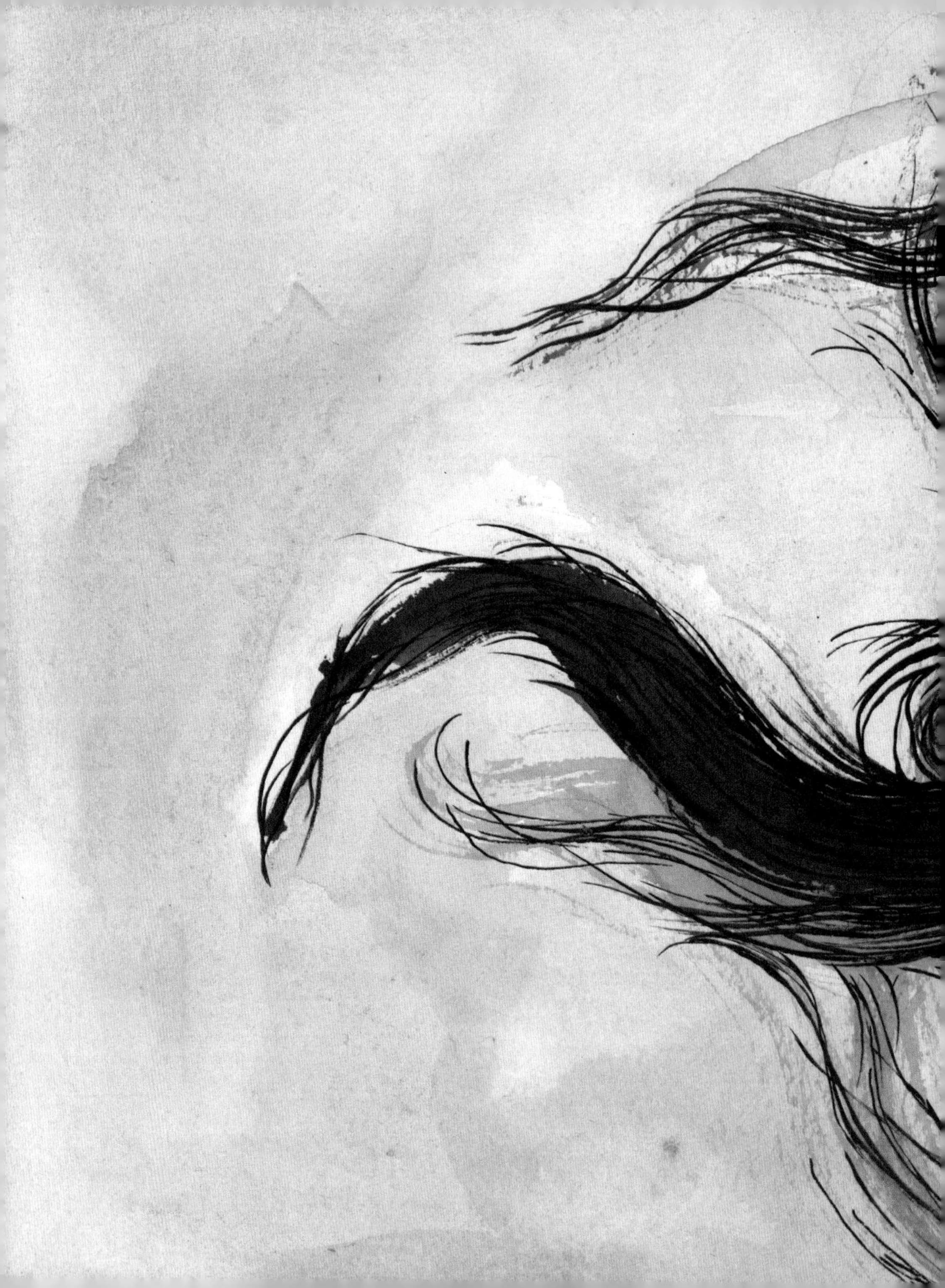

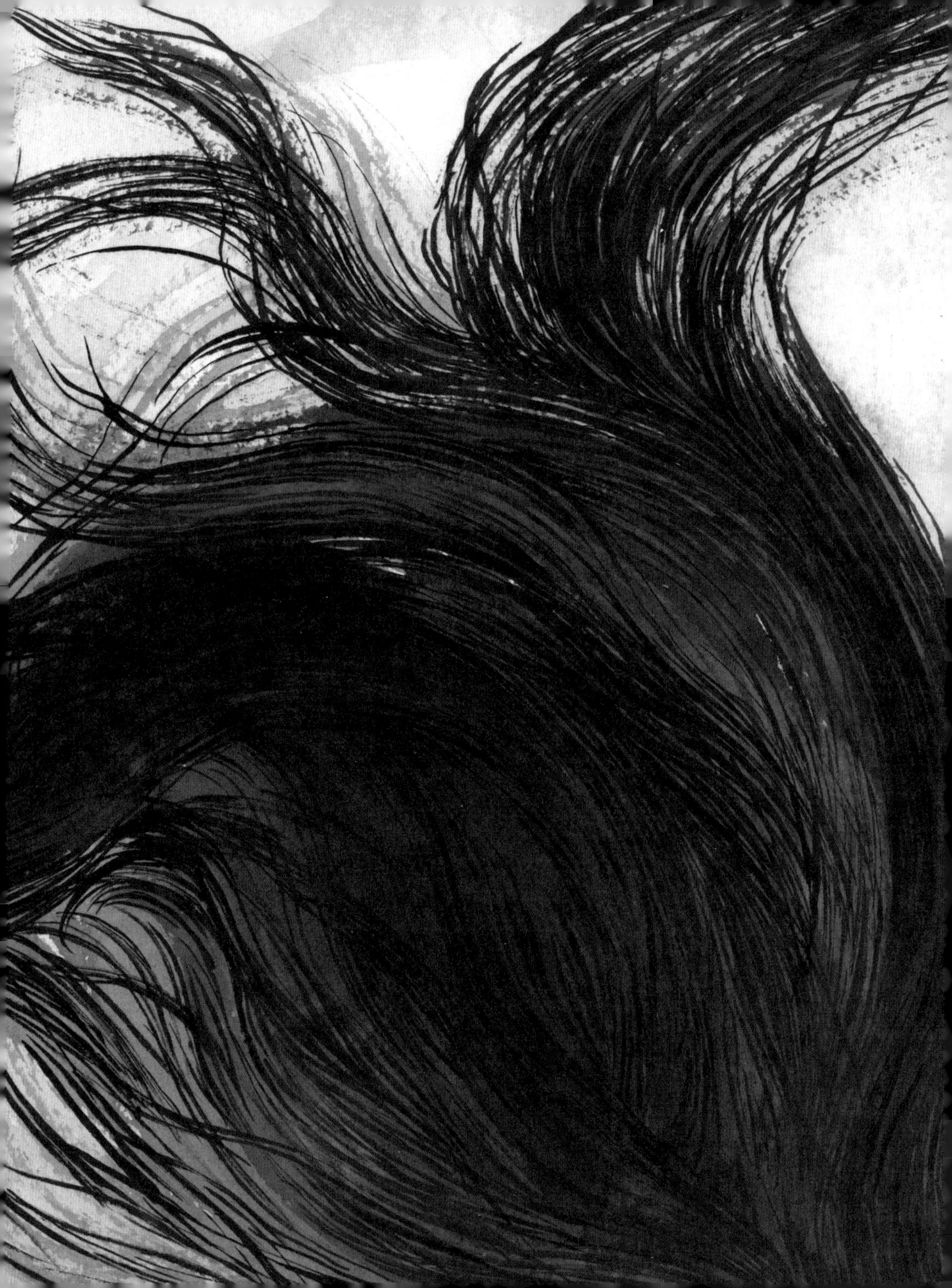

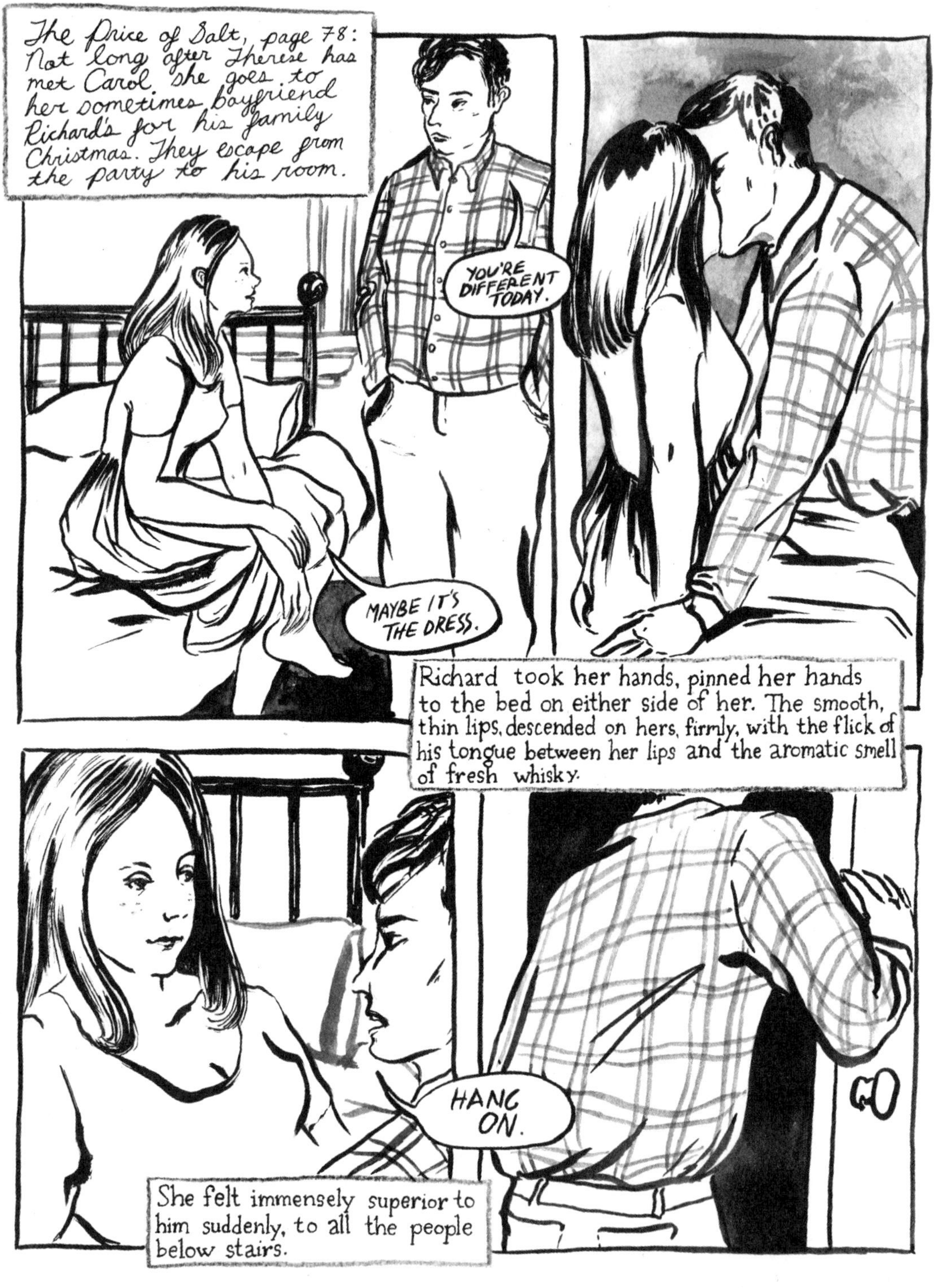
The Price of Salt, page 78: Not long after Therese has met Carol, she goes to her sometimes boyfriend Richard's for his family Christmas. They escape from the party to his room.
YOU'RE DIFFERENT TODAY.
MAYBE IT'S THE DRESS.
Richard took her hands, pinned her hands to the bed on either side of her. The smooth, thin lips, descended on hers, firmly, with the flick of his tongue between her lips and the aromatic smell of fresh whisky.
HANG ON.
She felt immensely superior to him suddenly, to all the people below stairs.

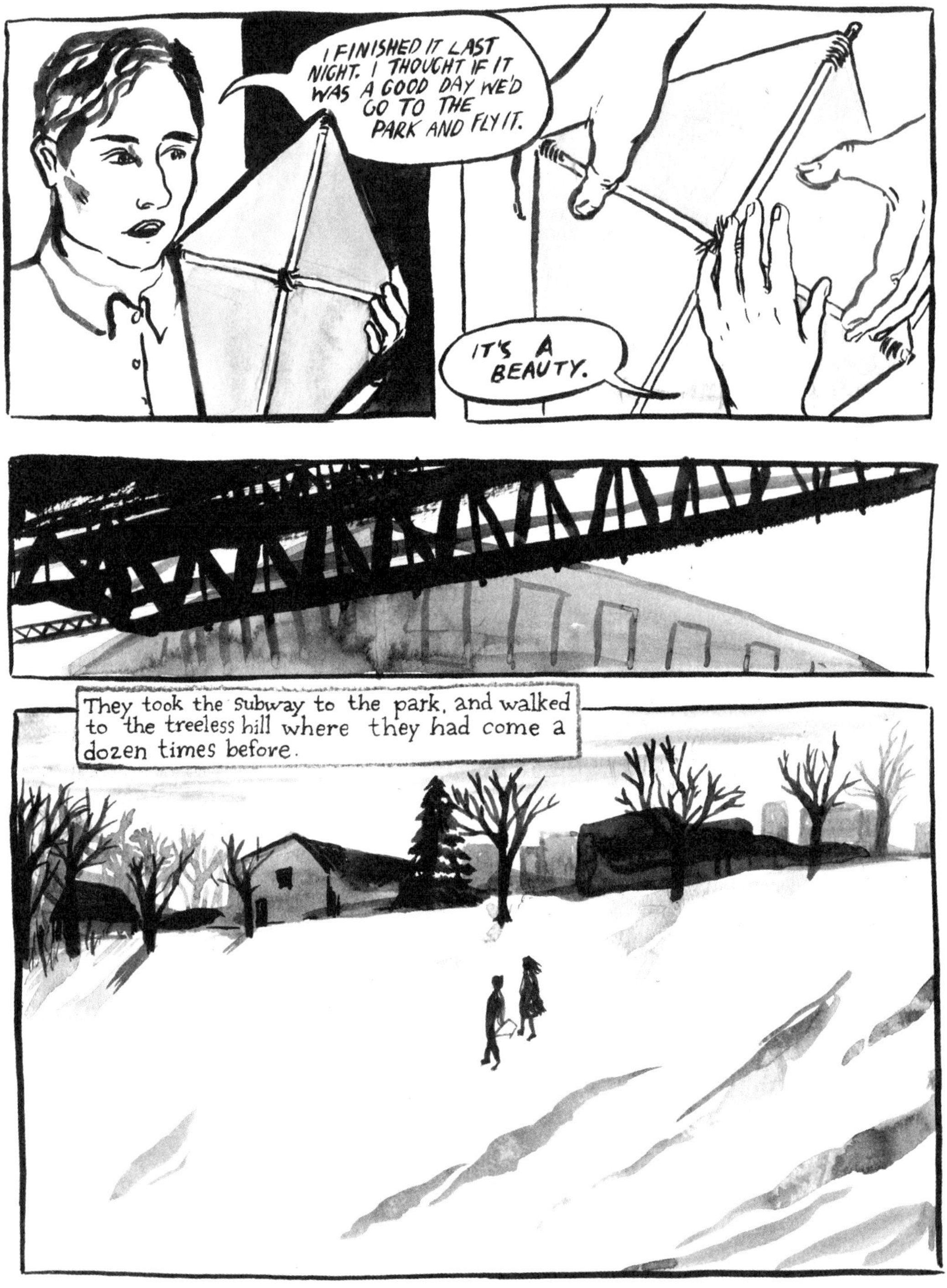
I FINISHED IT LAST NIGHT. I THOUGHT IF IT WAS A GOOD DAY WE'D GO TO THE PARK AND FLY IT.
IT'S A BEAUTY.
They took the subway to the park, and walked to the treeless hill where they had come a dozen times before.

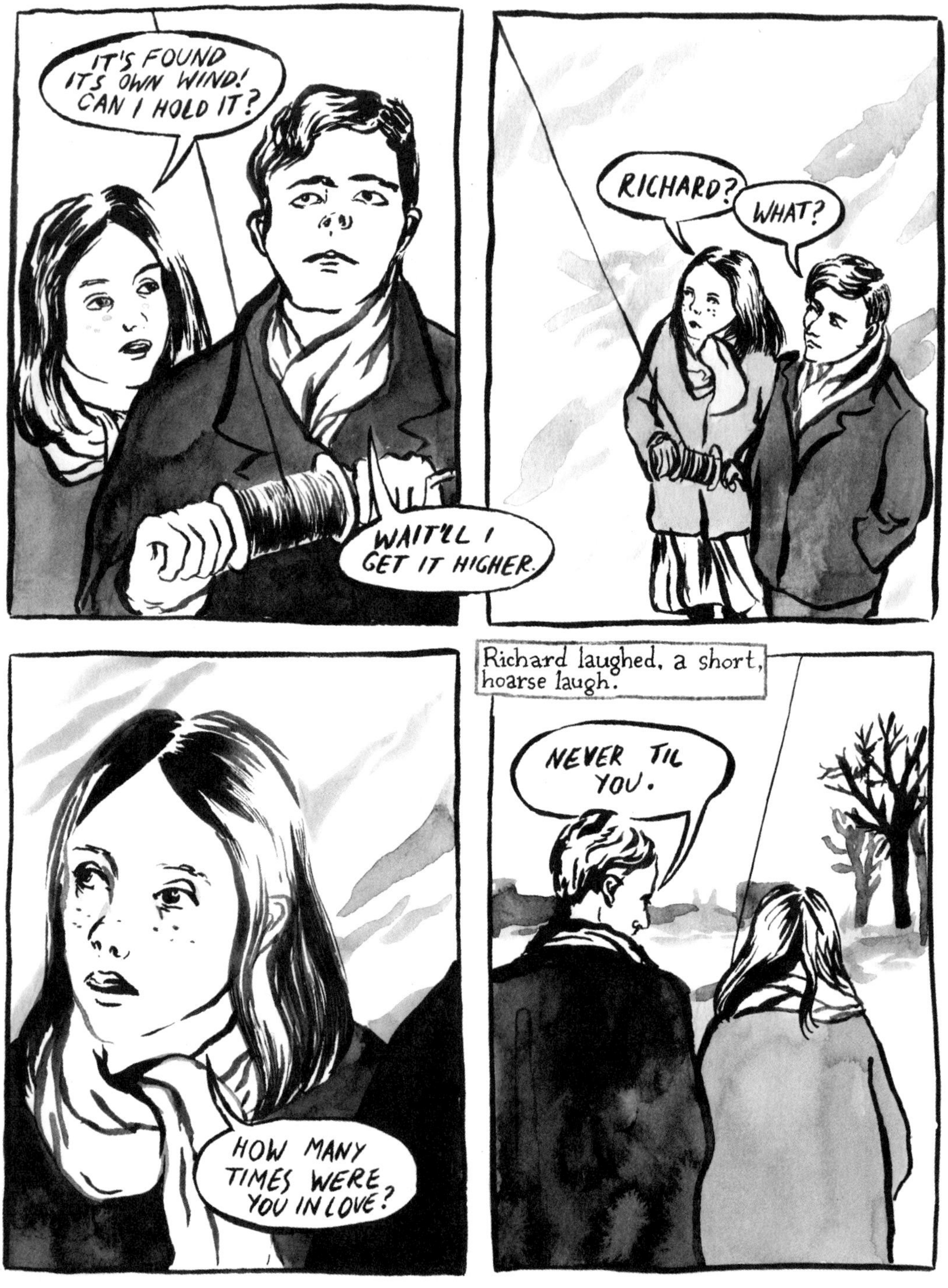
IT'S FOUND ITS OWN WIND! CAN I HOLD IT?
WAIT'LL I GET IT HIGHER.
RICHARD?
WHAT?
HOW MANY TIMES WERE YOU IN LOVE?
Richard laughed, a short, hoarse laugh.
NEVER TIL YOU.

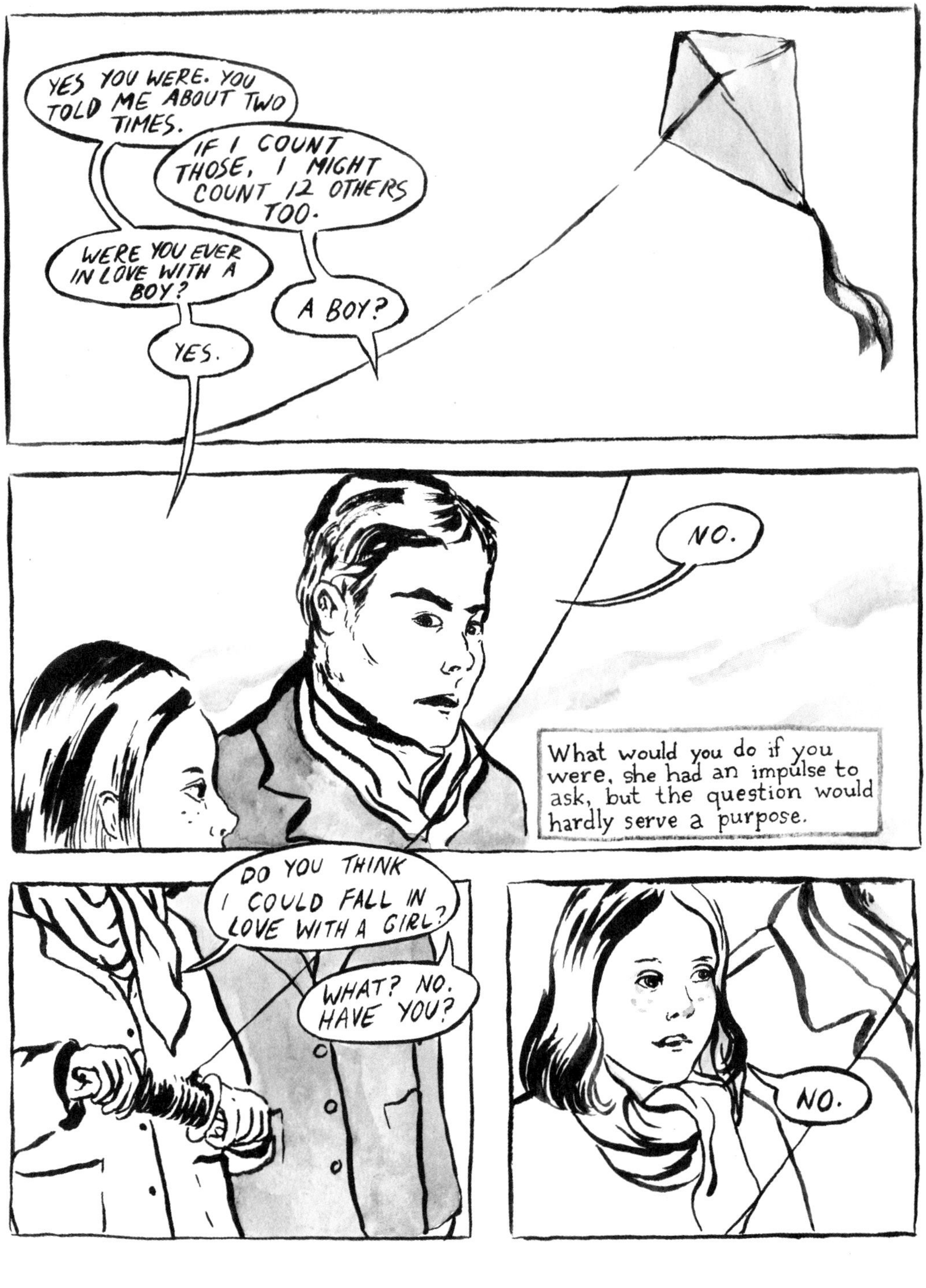
YES YOU WERE. YOU TOLD ME ABOUT TWO TIMES.
IF I COUNT THOSE, I MIGHT COUNT 12 OTHERS TOO.
WERE YOU EVER IN LOVE WITH A BOY?
A BOY?
YES.
NO.
What would you do if you were, she had an impulse to ask, but the question would hardly serve a purpose.
DO YOU THINK I COULD FALL IN LOVE WITH A GIRL?
WHAT? NO. HAVE YOU?
NO.

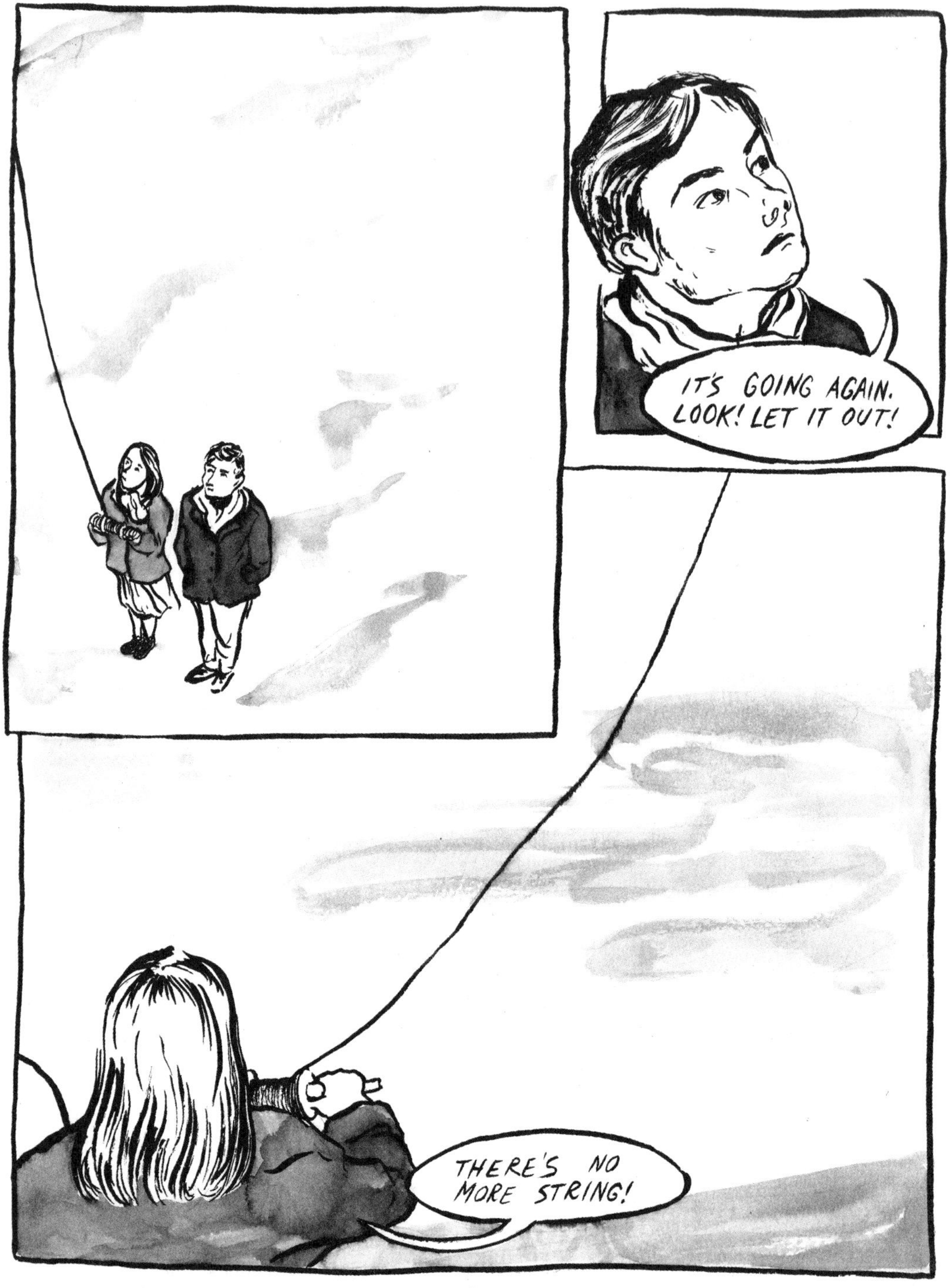
IT'S GOING AGAIN. LOOK! LET IT OUT!
THERE'S NO MORE STRING!

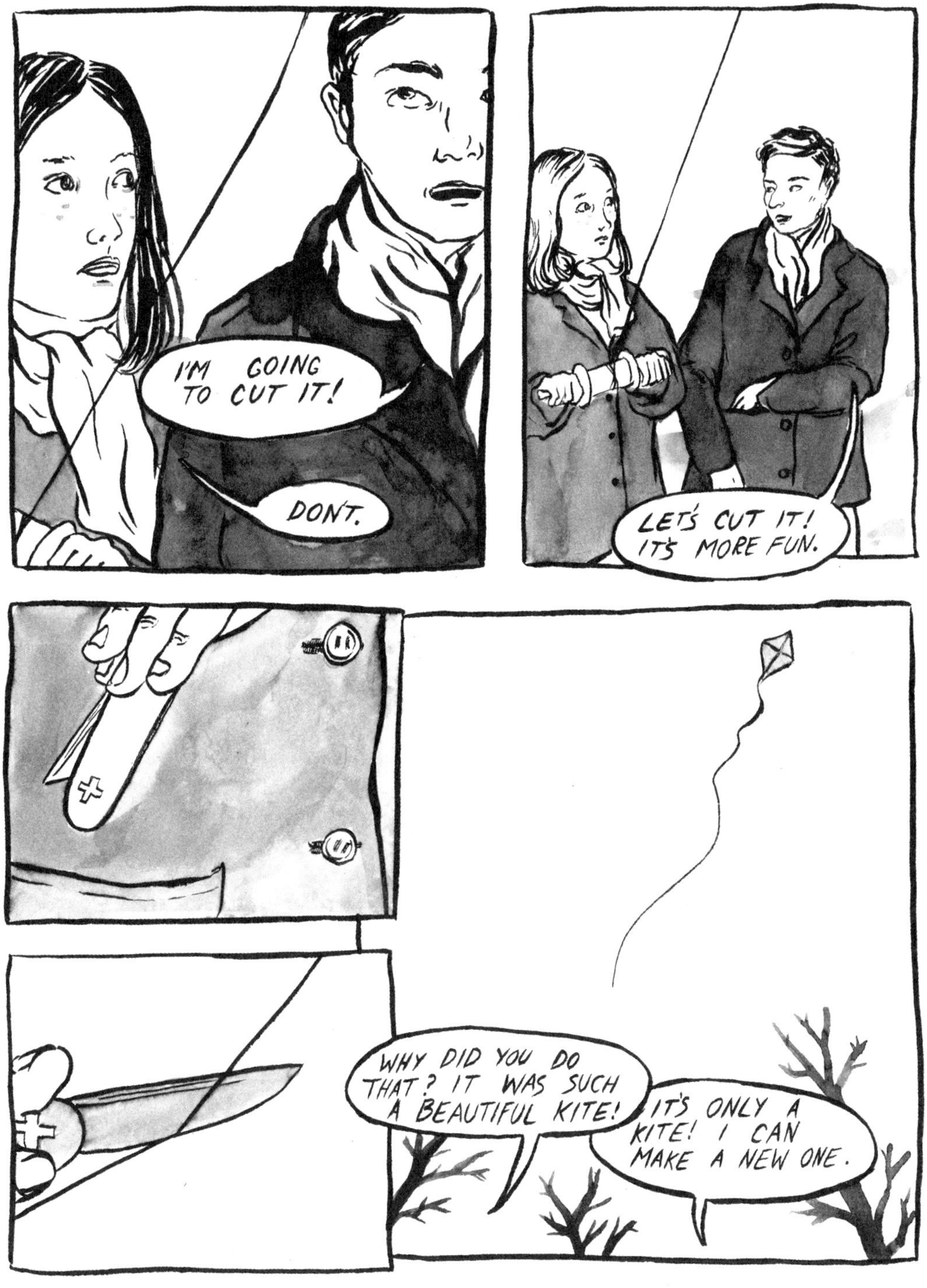
I'M GOING TO CUT IT!
DON'T.
LET'S CUT IT! IT'S MORE FUN.
WHY DID YOU DO THAT? IT WAS SUCH A BEAUTIFUL KITE!
IT'S ONLY A KITE! I CAN MAKE A NEW ONE.

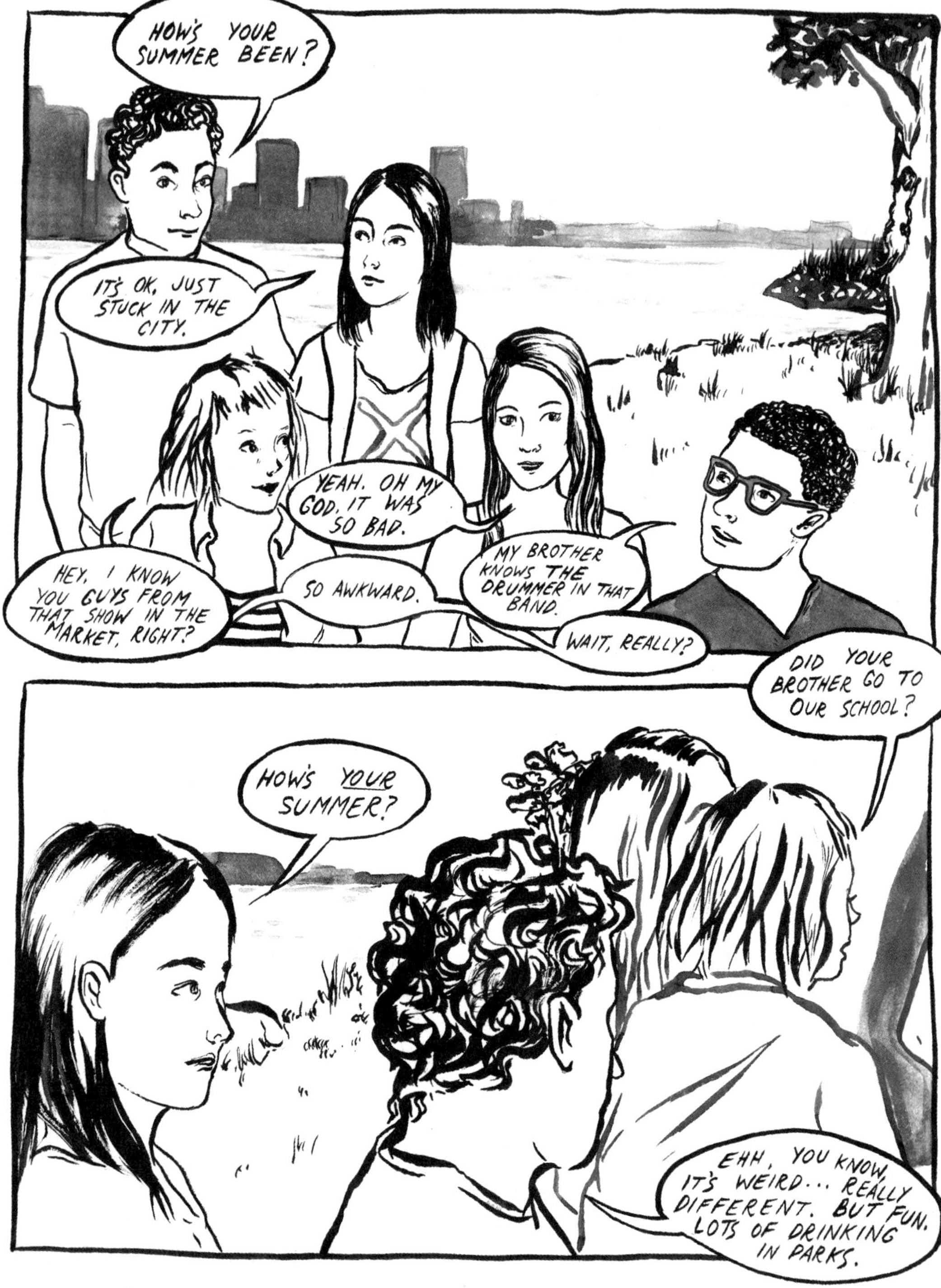
HOW'S YOUR SUMMER BEEN?
IT'S OK, JUST STUCK IN THE CITY.
YEAH. OH MY GOD, IT WAS SO BAD.
HEY, I KNOW YOU GUYS FROM THAT SHOW IN THE MARKET, RIGHT?
SO AWKWARD.
MY BROTHER KNOWS THE DRUMMER IN THAT BAND.
WAIT, REALLY?
DID YOUR BROTHER GO TO OUR SCHOOL?
HOW'S YOUR SUMMER?
EHH, YOU KNOW, IT'S WEIRD... REALLY DIFFERENT. BUT FUN. LOTS OF DRINKING IN PARKS.

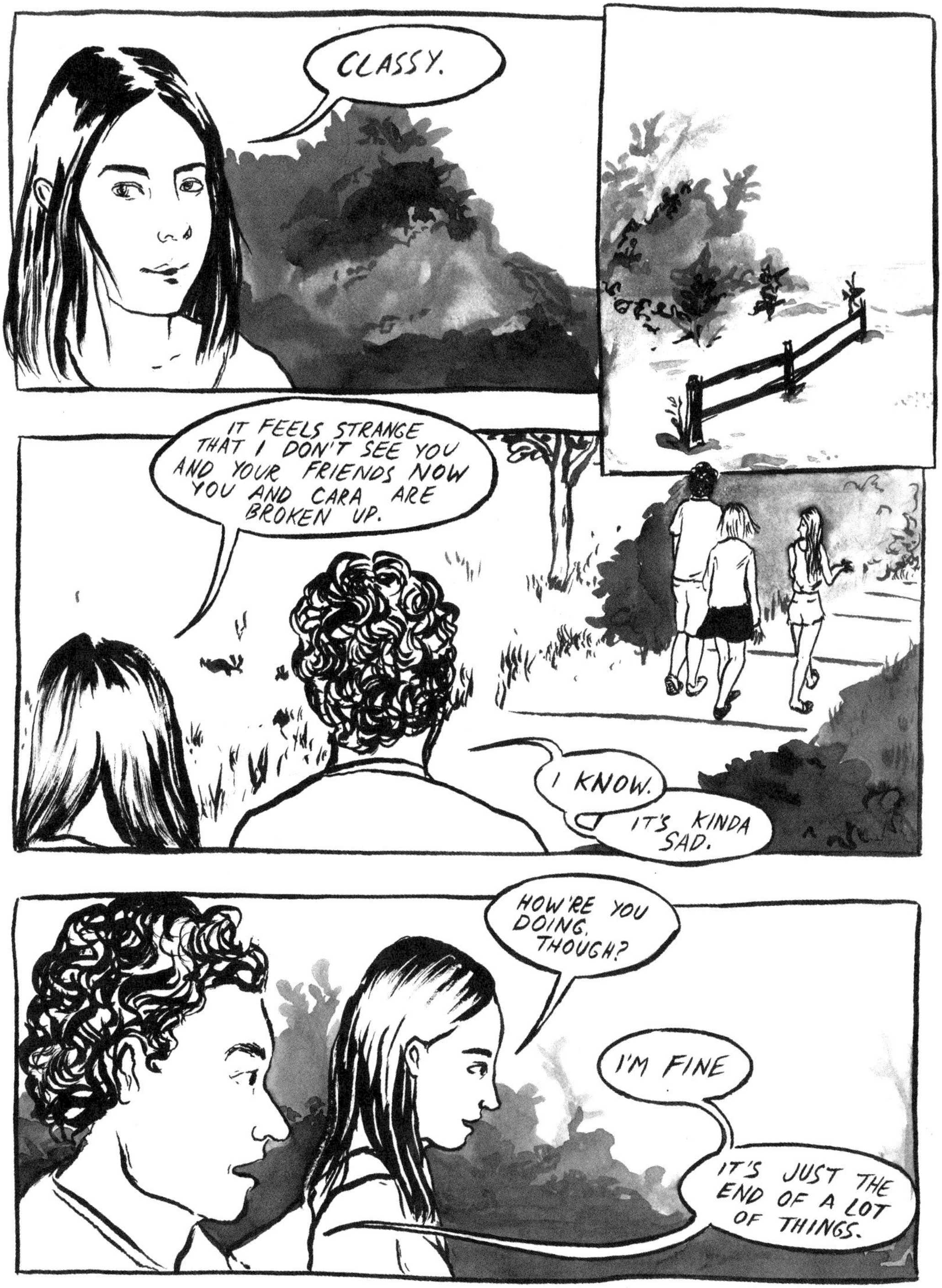
CLASSY.
IT FEELS STRANGE THAT I DON'T SEE YOU AND YOUR FRIENDS NOW YOU AND CARA ARE BROKEN UP.
I KNOW.
IT'S KINDA SAD.
HOW'RE YOU DOING, THOUGH?
I'M FINE
IT'S JUST THE END OF A LOT OF THINGS.

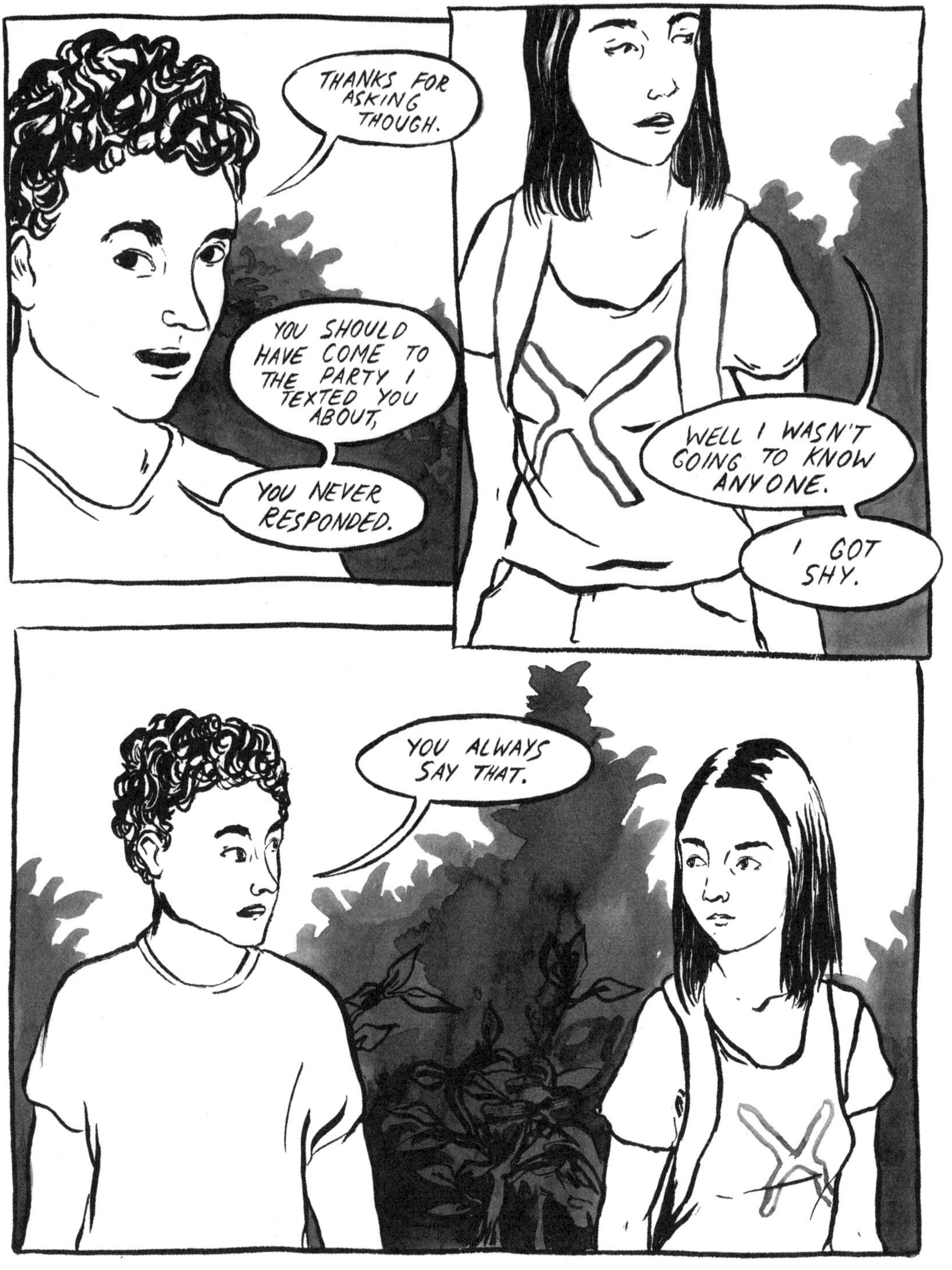
THANKS FOR ASKING THOUGH.
YOU SHOULD HAVE COME TO THE PARTY I TEXTED YOU ABOUT,
YOU NEVER RESPONDED.
WELL I WASN'T GOING TO KNOW ANYONE.
I GOT SHY.
YOU ALWAYS SAY THAT.

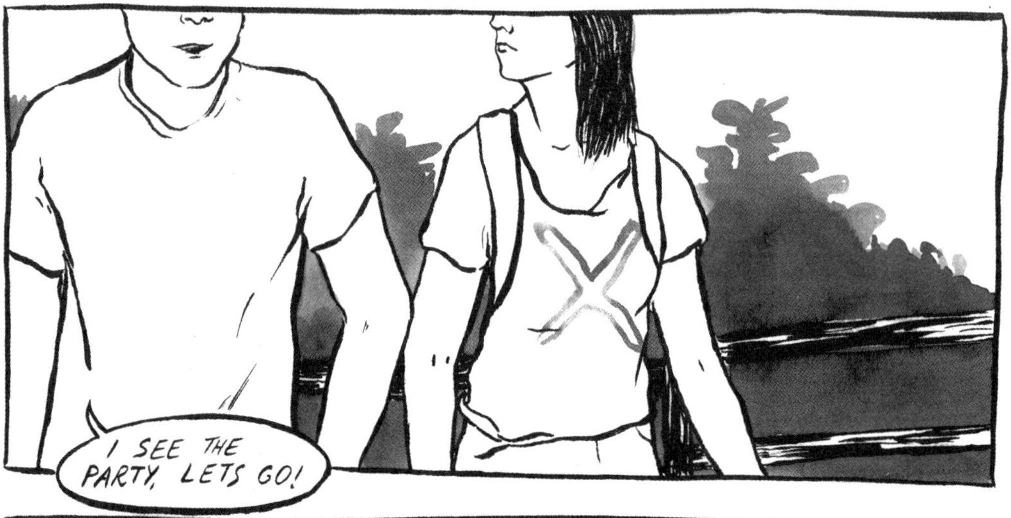
I SEE THE PARTY, LETS GO!

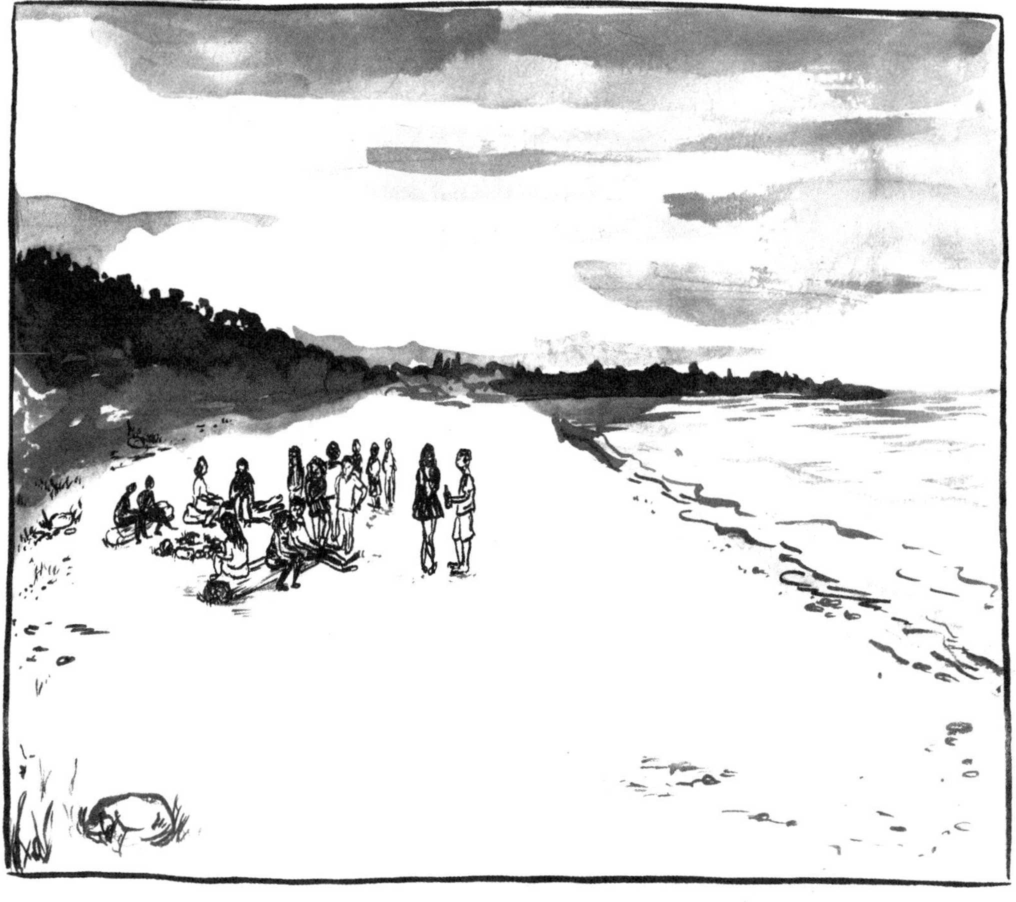

To The Lighthouse, page 131

Now all the candles were lit, and the faces on both sides of the table were brought nearer by the candle light, and composed, as they had not been in the twilight, into a party round a table, for the night was now shut off by panes of glass, which, far from giving any accurate view of the outside world, rippled it so strangely that here, inside the room, seemed to be order and dry land; there, outside, a reflection in which things wavered and vanished, waterily.

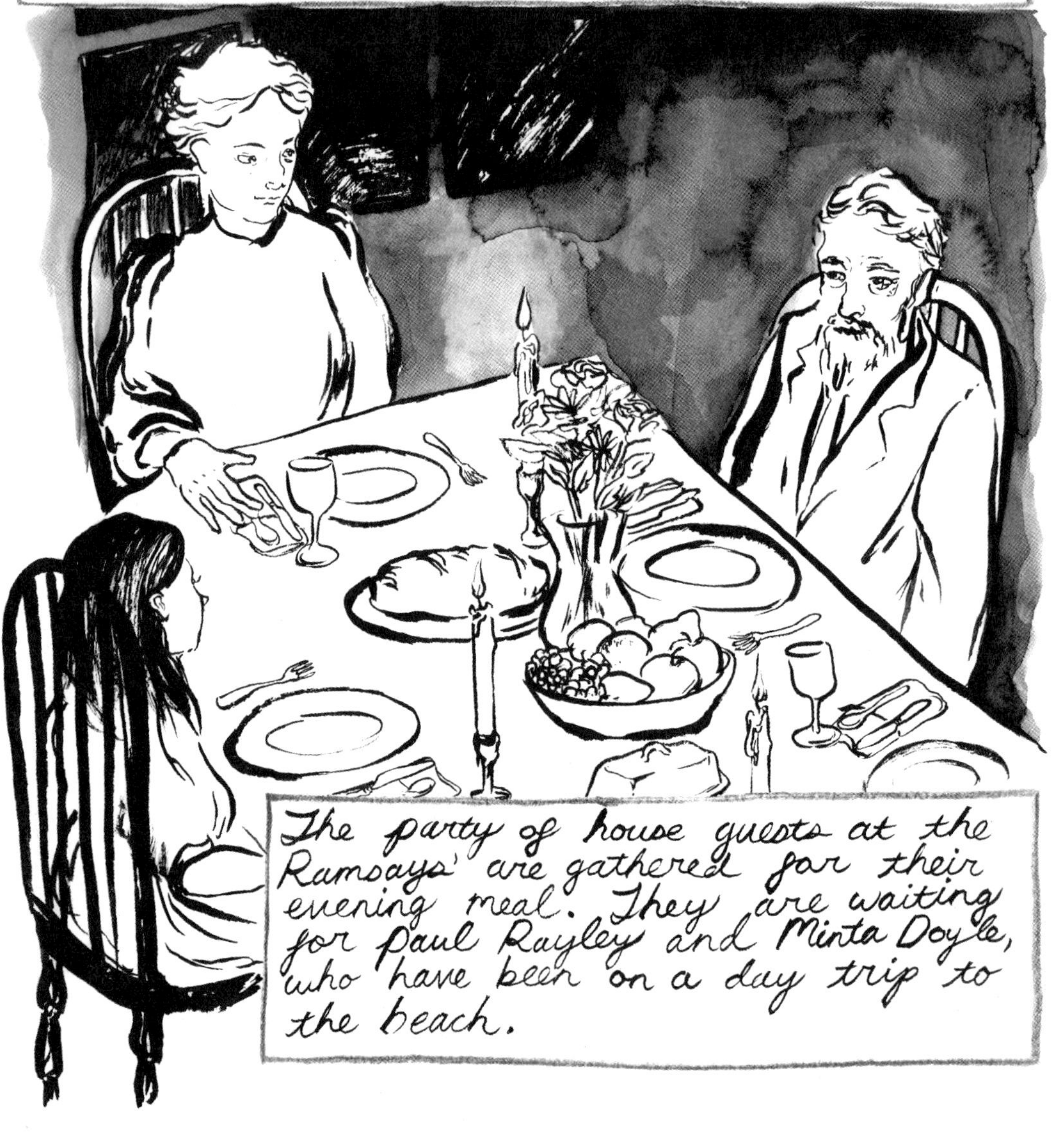
The party of house guests at the Ramsays' are gathered for their evening meal. They are waiting for Paul Rayley and Minta Doyle, who have been on a day trip to the beach.

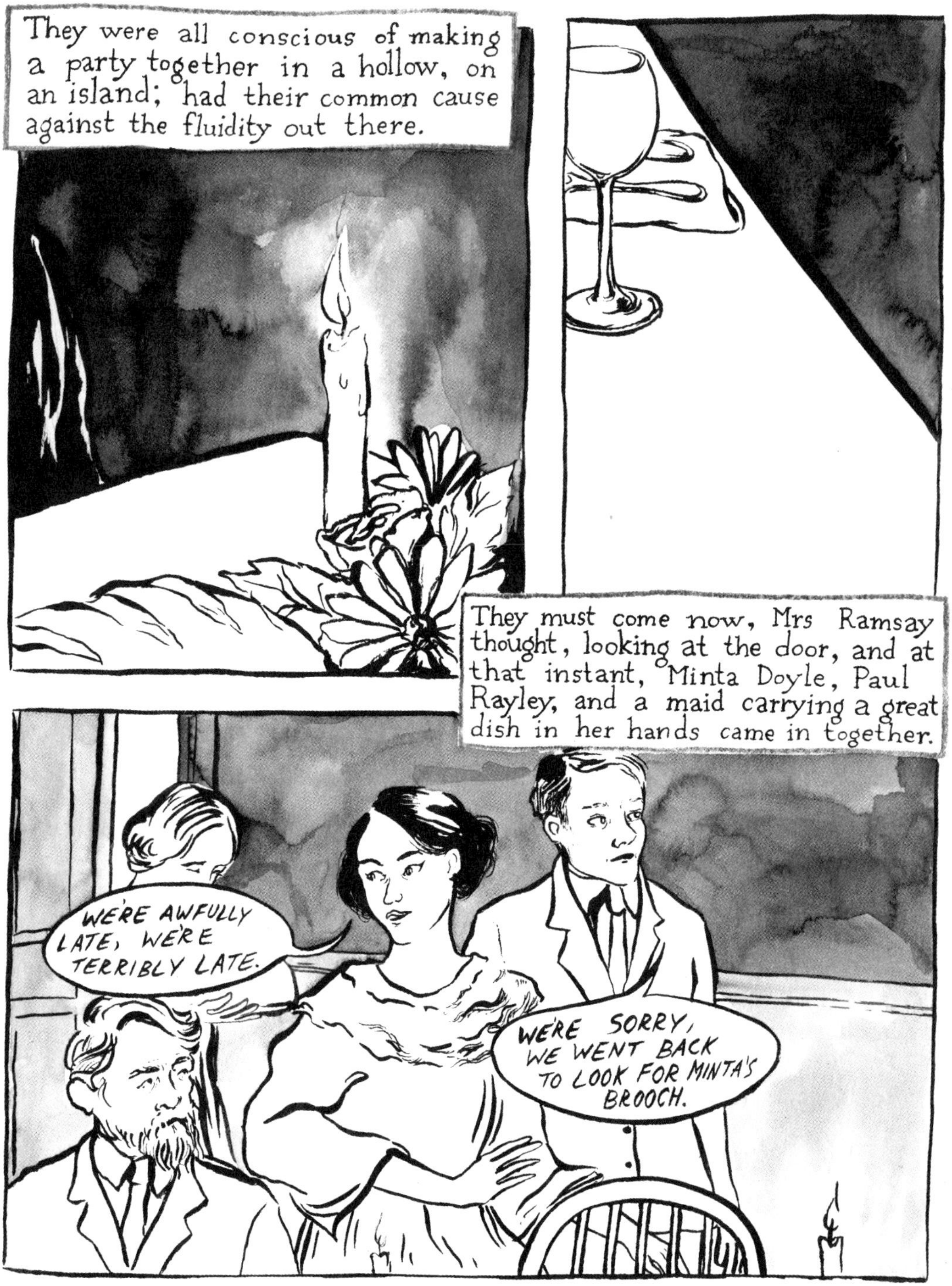
They were all conscious of making a party together in a hollow, on an island; had their common cause against the fluidity out there.
They must come now, Mrs Ramsay thought, looking at the door, and at that instant, Minta Doyle, Paul Rayley, and a maid carrying a great dish in her hands came in together.
WE'RE AWFULLY LATE, WE'RE TERRIBLY LATE.
WE'RE SORRY, WE WENT BACK TO LOOK FOR MINTA'S BROOCH.

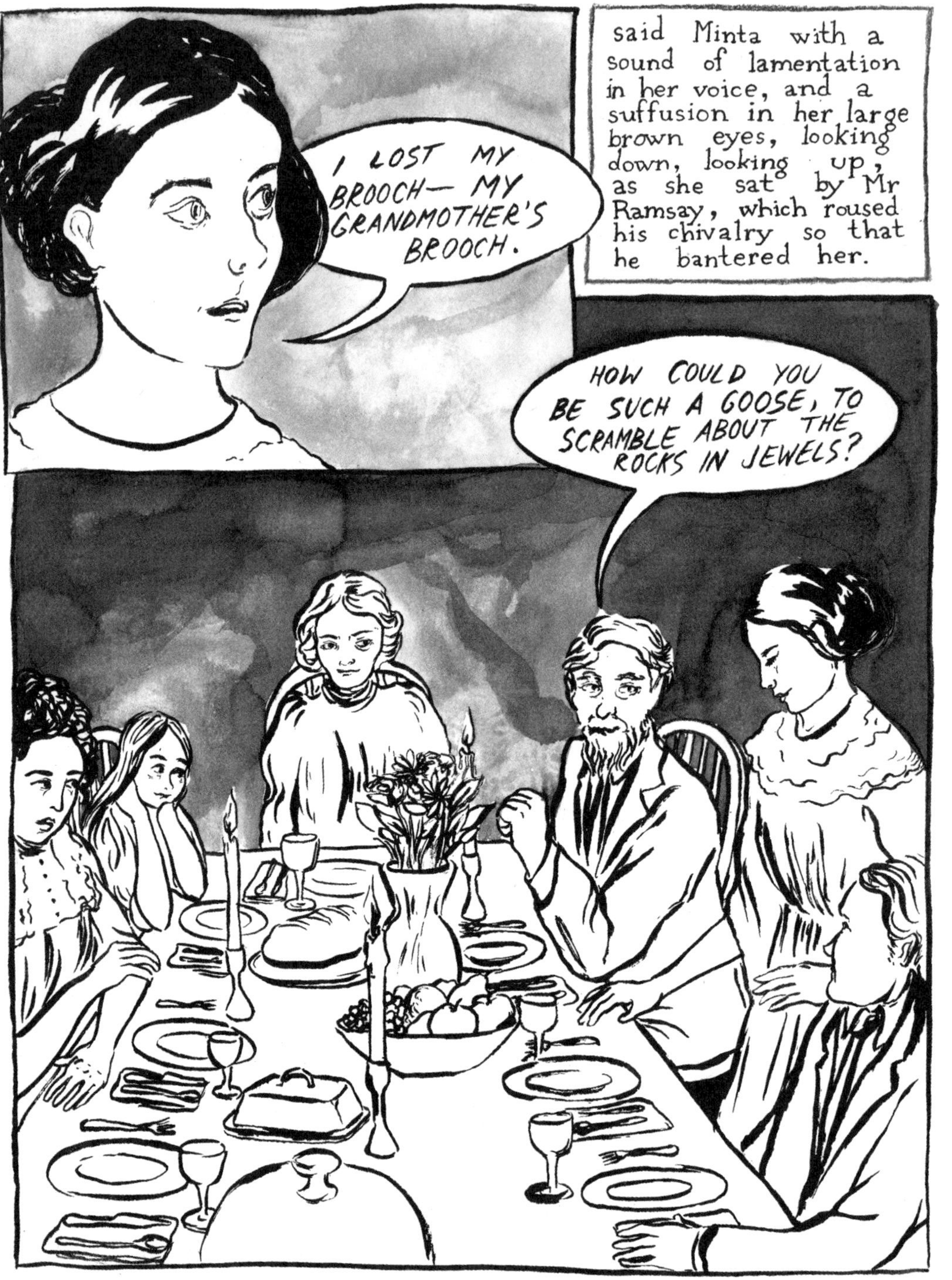
I LOST MY BROOCH— MY GRANDMOTHER'S BROOCH.
said Minta with a sound of lamentation in her voice, and a suffusion in her large brown eyes, looking down, looking up, as she sat by Mr Ramsay, which roused his chivalry so that he bantered her.
HOW COULD YOU BE SUCH A GOOSE, TO SCRAMBLE ABOUT THE ROCKS IN JEWELS?

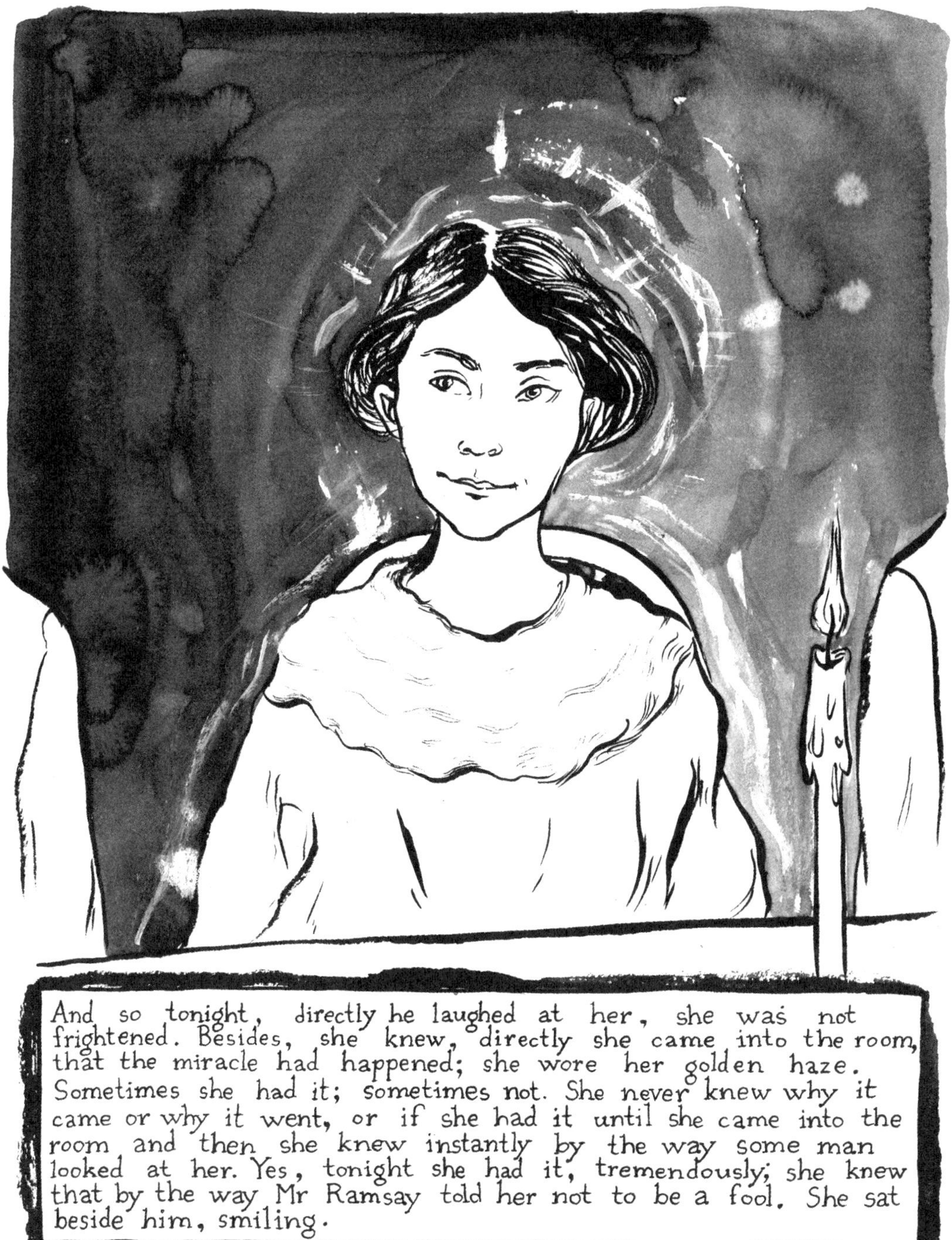
And so tonight, directly he laughed at her, she was not frightened. Besides, she knew, directly she came into the room, that the miracle had happened; she wore her golden haze. Sometimes she had it; sometimes not. She never knew why it came or why it went, or if she had it until she came into the room and then she knew instantly by the way some man looked at her. Yes, tonight she had it, tremendously; she knew that by the way Mr Ramsay told her not to be a fool. She sat beside him, smiling.

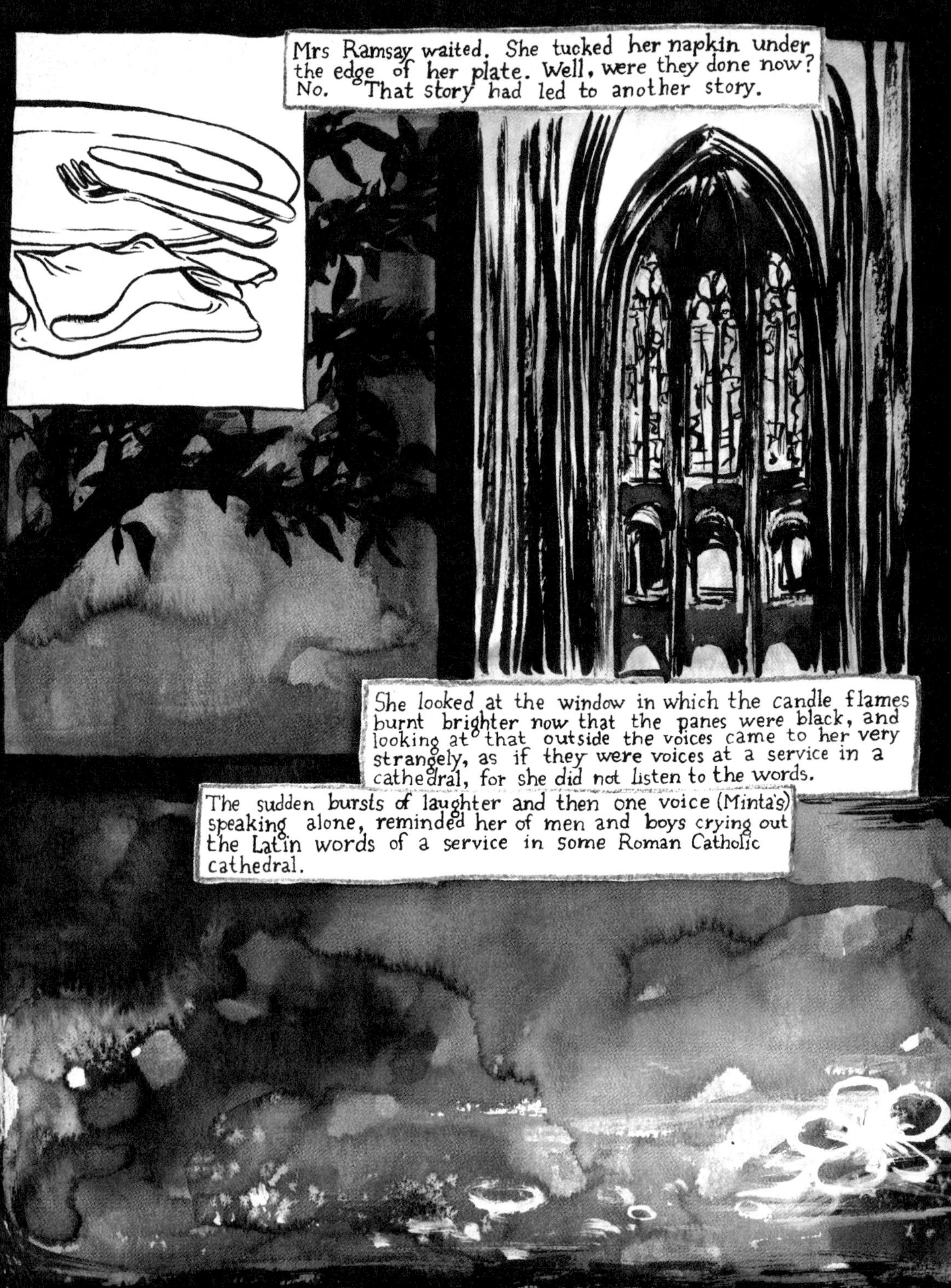
Mrs Ramsay waited. She tucked her napkin under the edge of her plate. Well, were they done now? No. That story had led to another story.
She looked at the window in which the candle flames burnt brighter now that the panes were black, and looking at that outside the voices came to her very strangely, as if they were voices at a service in a cathedral, for she did not listen to the words.
The sudden bursts of laughter and then one voice (Minta's) speaking alone, reminded her of men and boys crying out the Latin words of a service in some Roman Catholic cathedral.

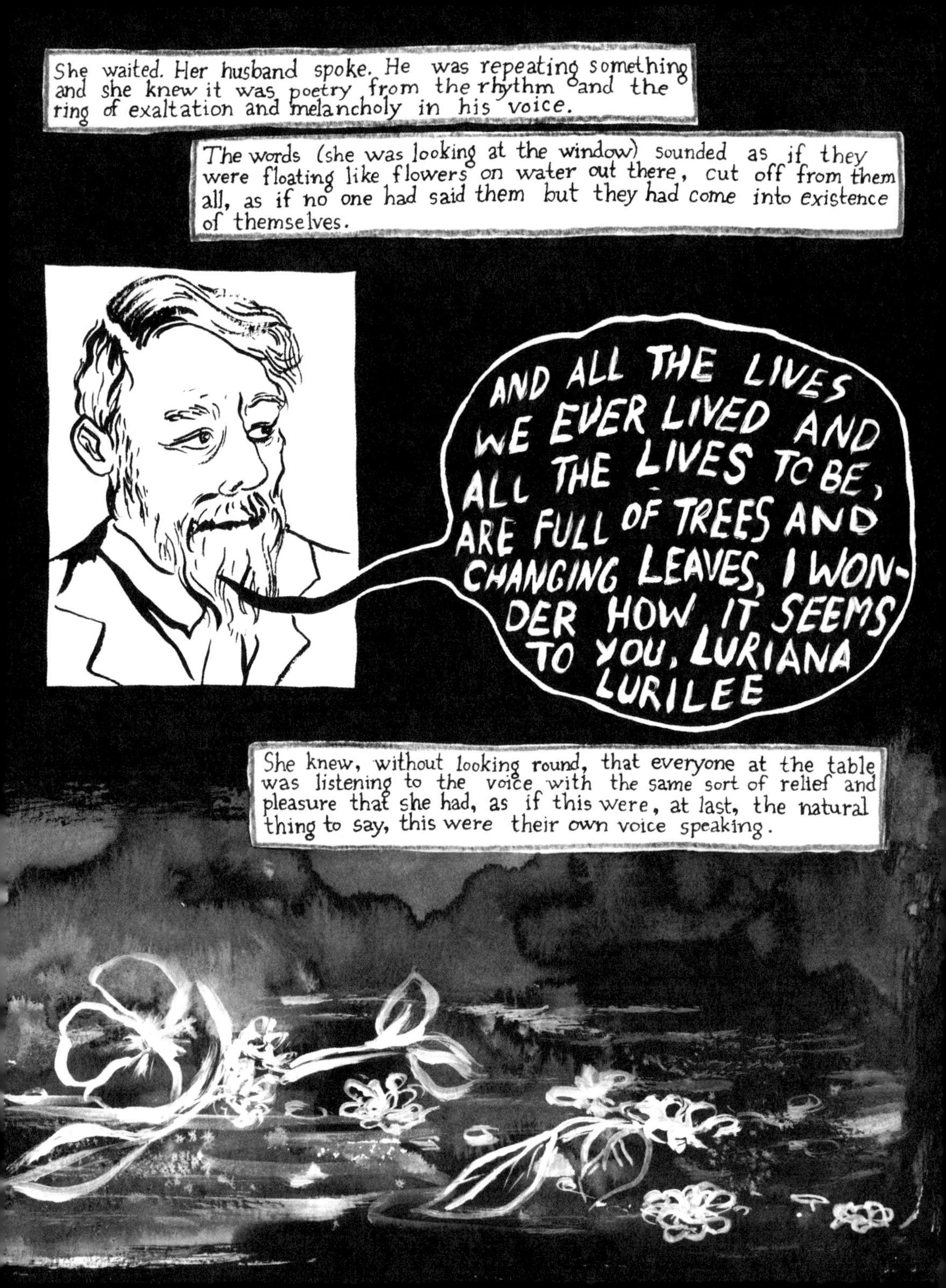
She waited. Her husband spoke. He was repeating something and she knew it was poetry from the rhythm and the ring of exaltation and melancholy in his voice.
The words (she was looking at the window) sounded as if they were floating like flowers on water out there, cut off from them all, as if no one had said them but they had come into existence of themselves.
AND ALL THE LIVES WE EVER LIVED AND ALL THE LIVES TO BE, ARE FULL OF TREES AND CHANGING LEAVES, I WONDER HOW IT SEEMS TO YOU, LURIANA LURILEE
She knew, without looking round, that everyone at the table was listening to the voice with the same sort of relief and pleasure that she had, as if this were, at last, the natural thing to say, this were their own voice speaking.

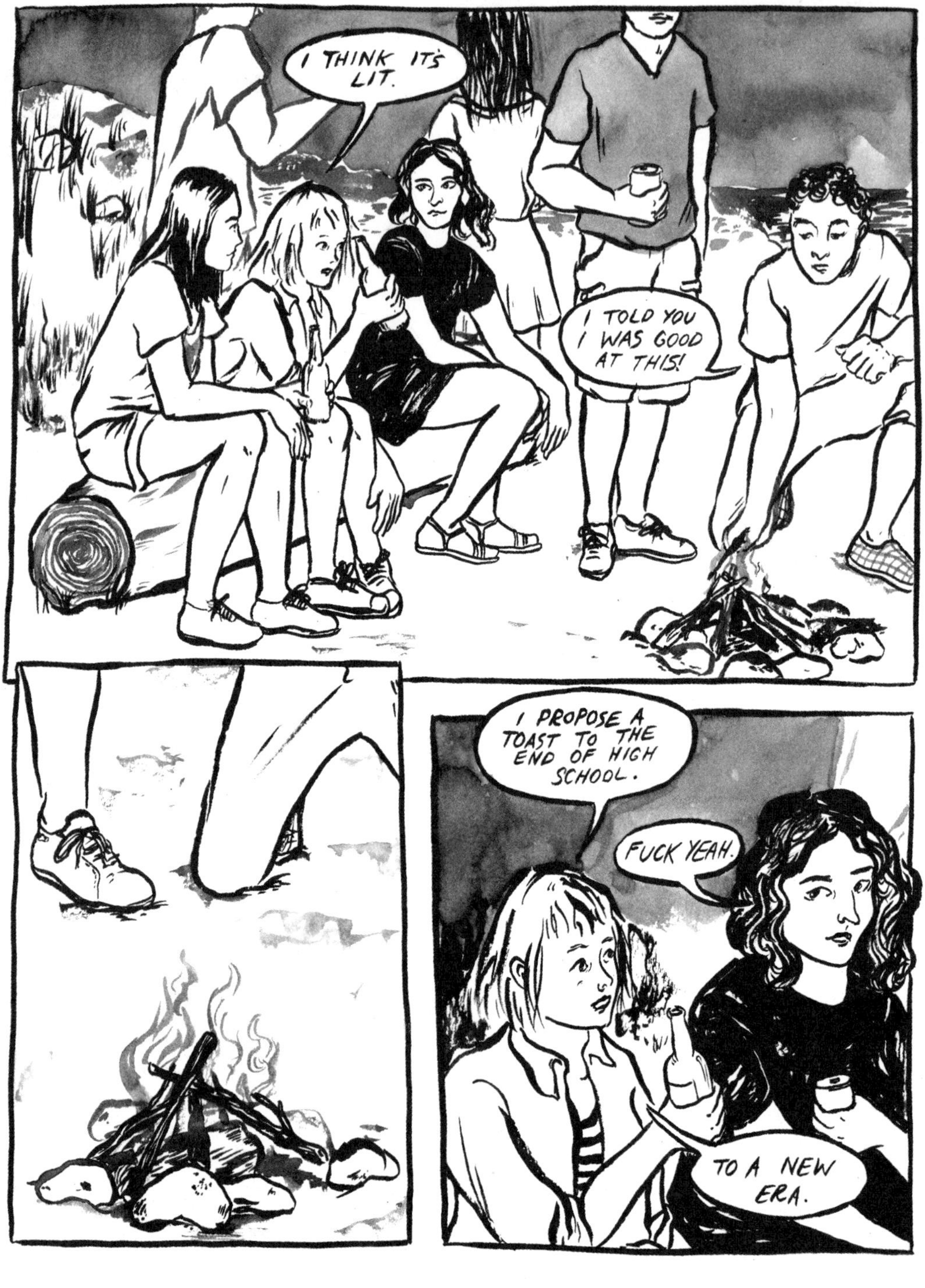
I THINK IT'S LIT.
I TOLD YOU I WAS GOOD AT THIS!
I PROPOSE A TOAST TO THE END OF HIGH SCHOOL.
FUCK YEAH.
TO A NEW ERA.

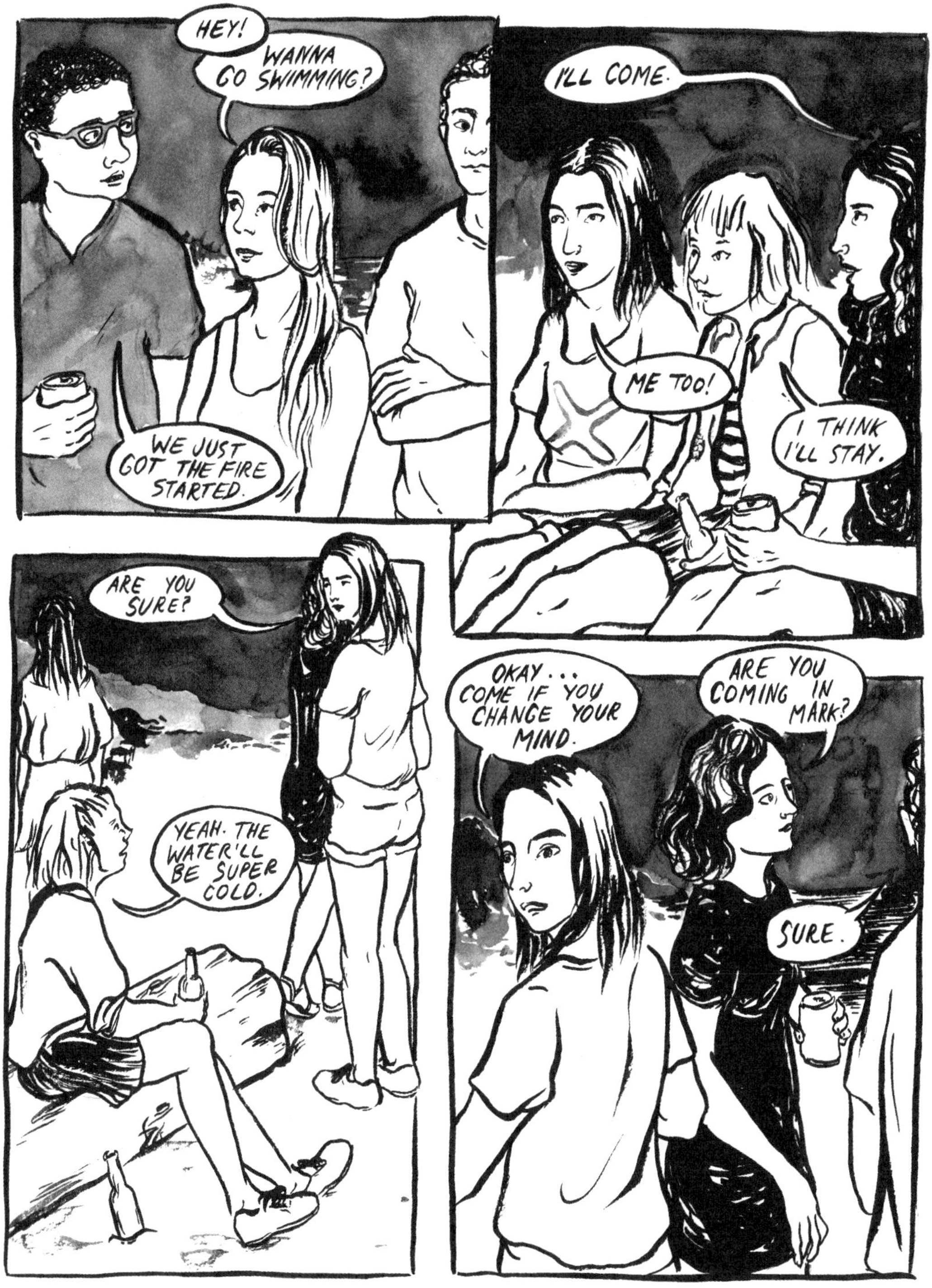
HEY!
WANNA GO SWIMMING?
WE JUST GOT THE FIRE STARTED.
I'LL COME.
ME TOO!
I THINK I'LL STAY.
ARE YOU SURE?
YEAH. THE WATER'LL BE SUPER COLD.
OKAY... COME IF YOU CHANGE YOUR MIND.
ARE YOU COMING IN MARK?
SURE.

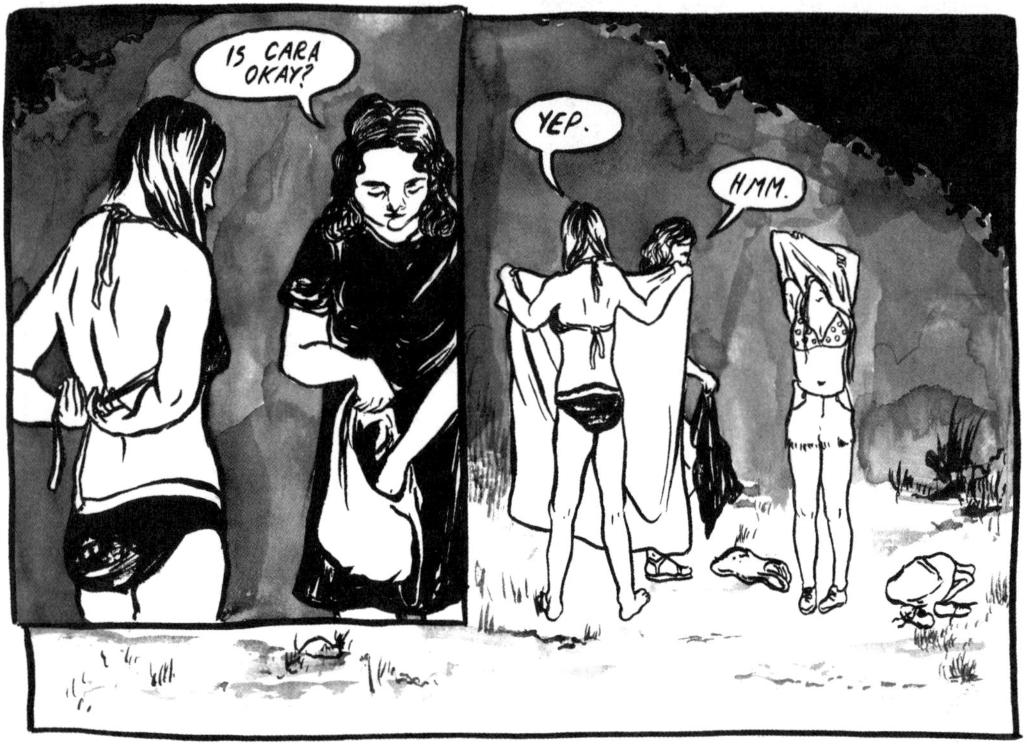
IS CARA OKAY?
YEP.
HMM.

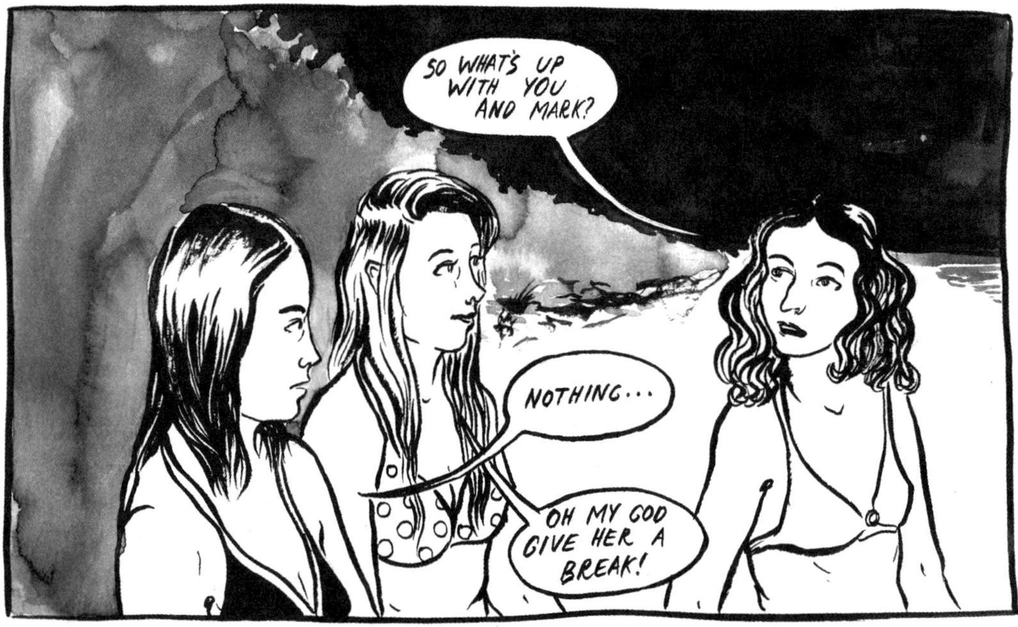
SO WHAT'S UP WITH YOU AND MARK?
NOTHING...
OH MY GOD GIVE HER A BREAK!

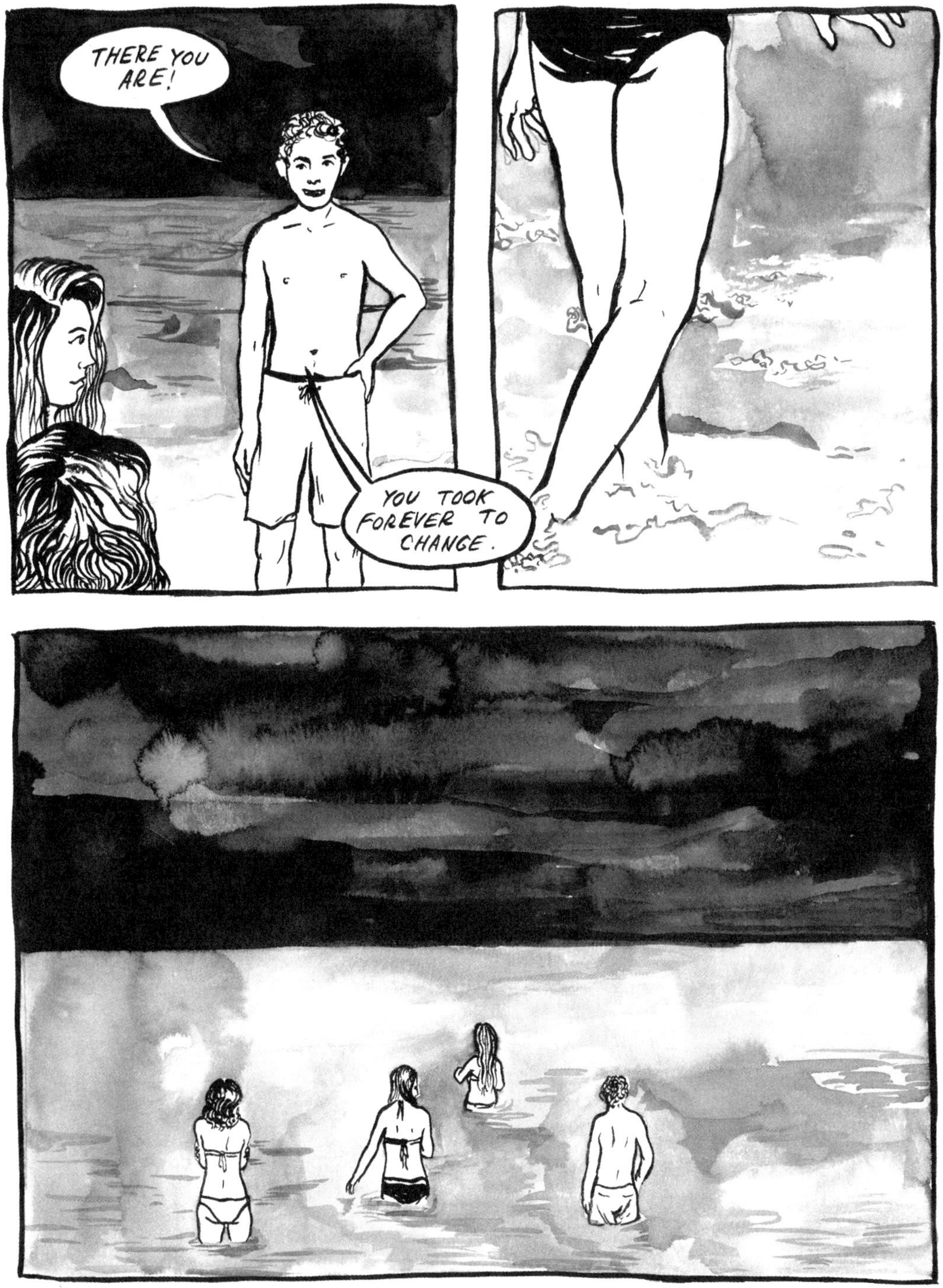
THERE YOU ARE!
YOU TOOK FOREVER TO CHANGE.

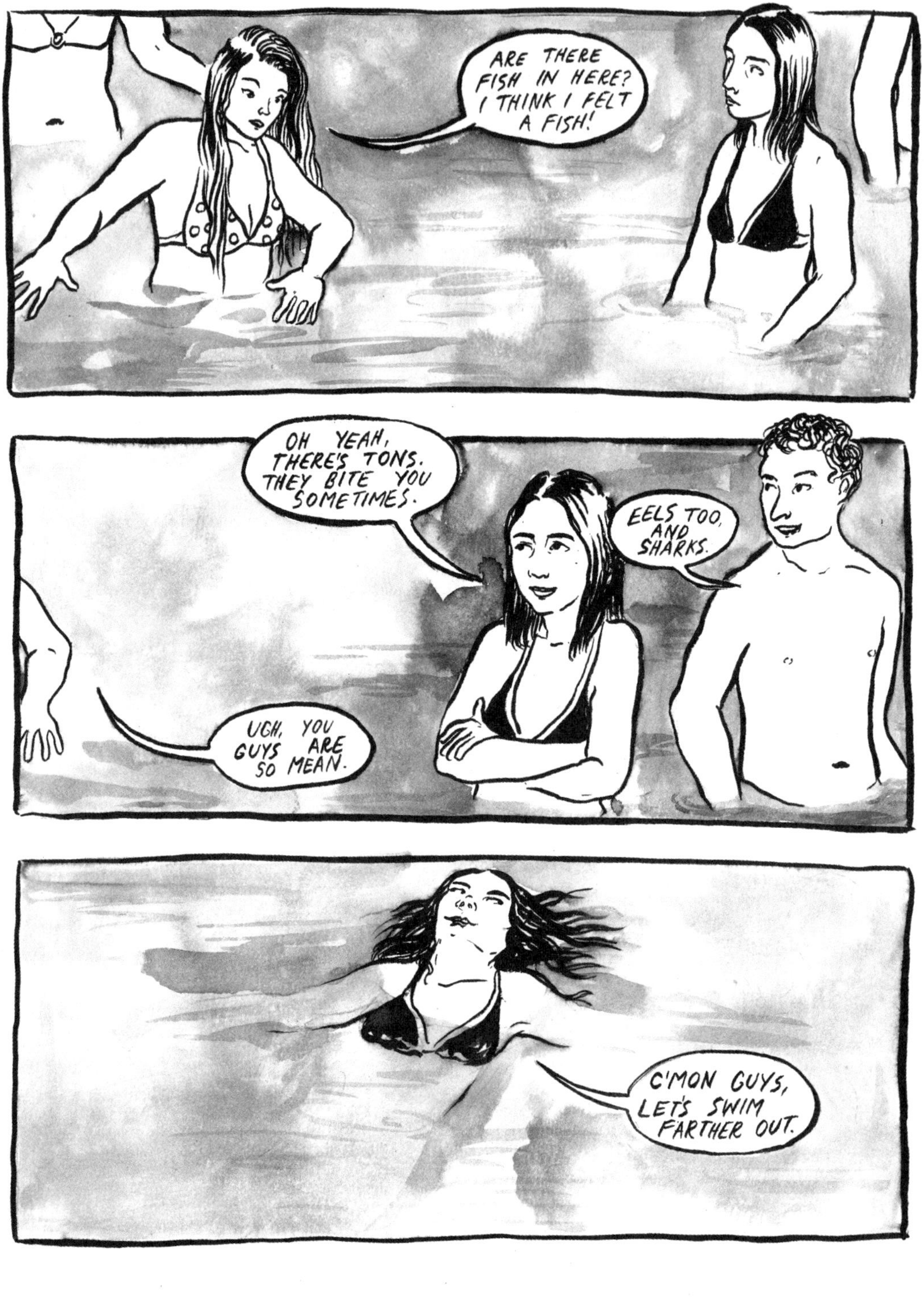
ARE THERE FISH IN HERE? I THINK I FELT A FISH!
OH YEAH, THERE'S TONS. THEY BITE YOU SOMETIMES.
EELS TOO, AND SHARKS.
UGH, YOU GUYS ARE SO MEAN.
C'MON GUYS, LET'S SWIM FARTHER OUT.

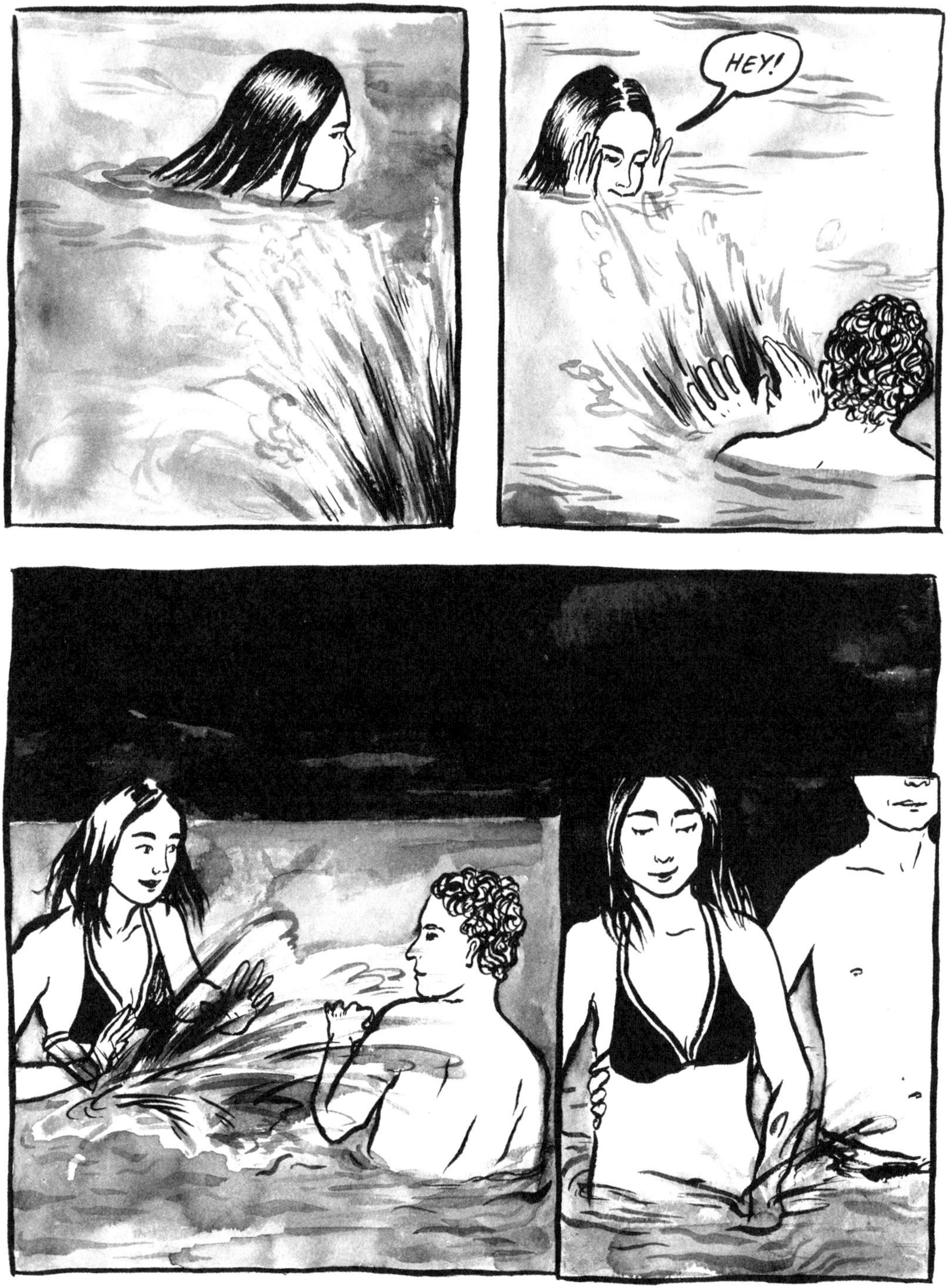
HEY!

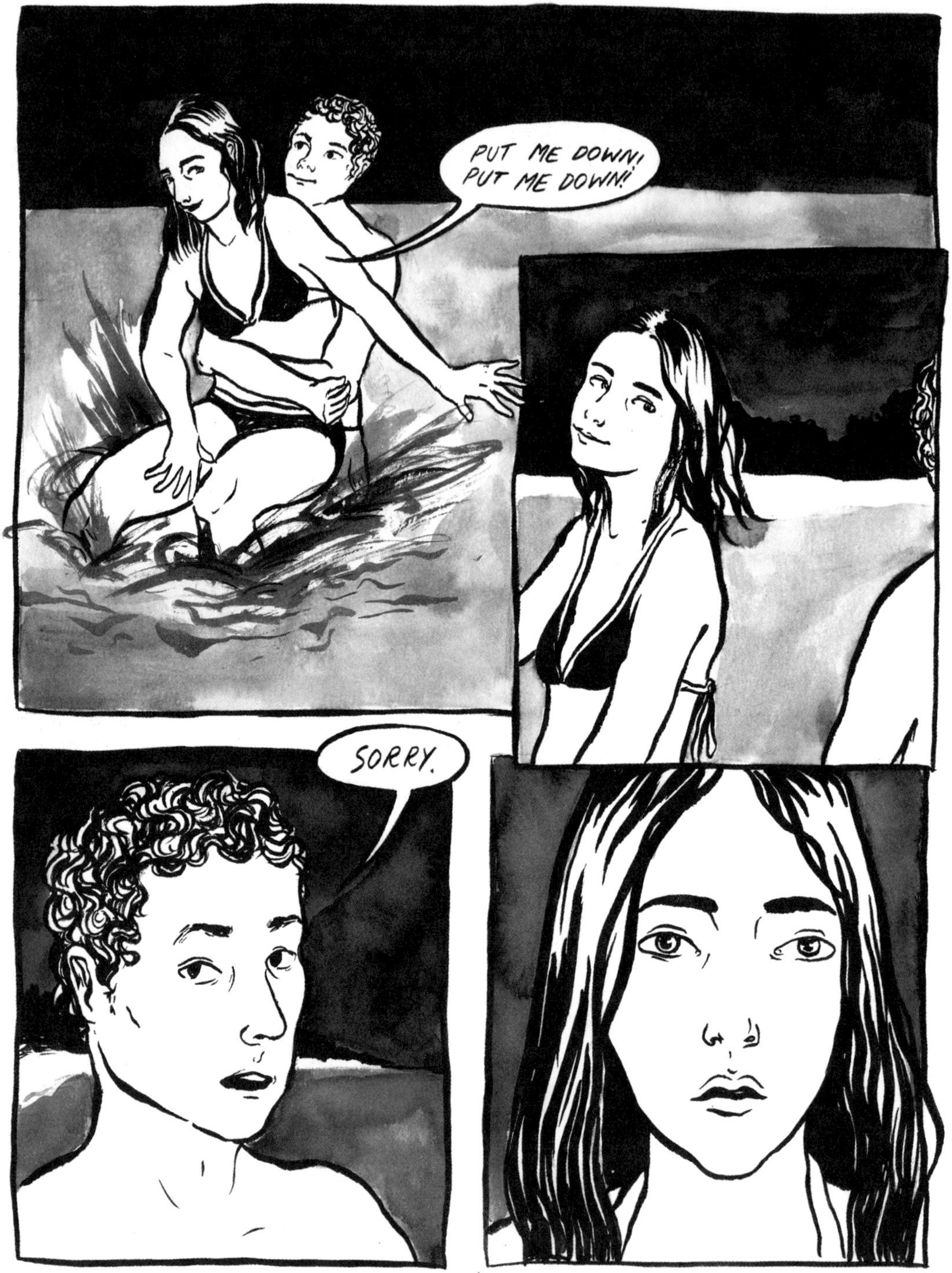
PUT ME DOWN! PUT ME DOWN!
SORRY.

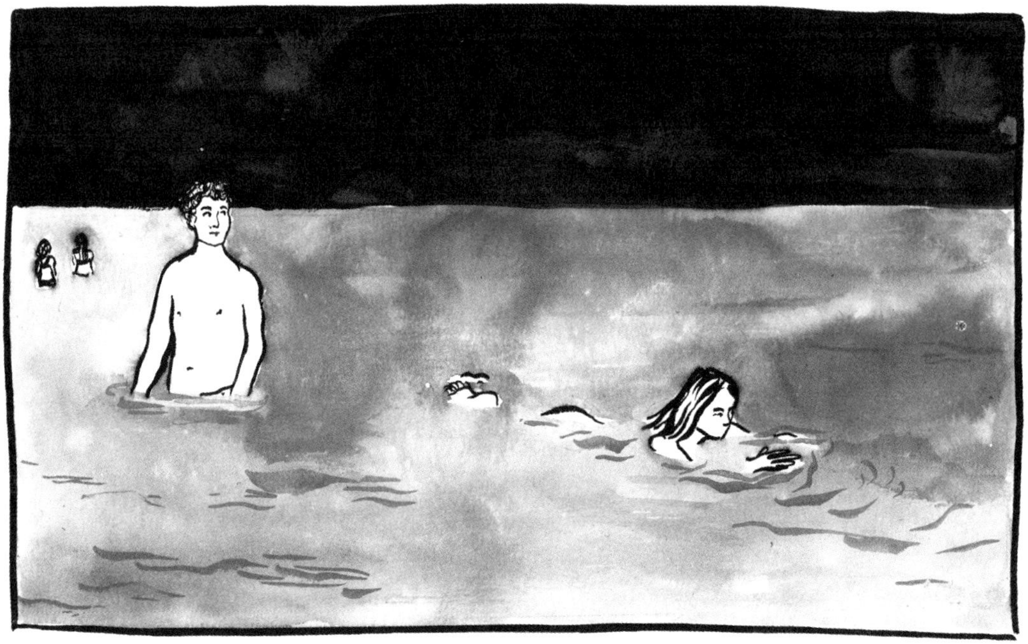

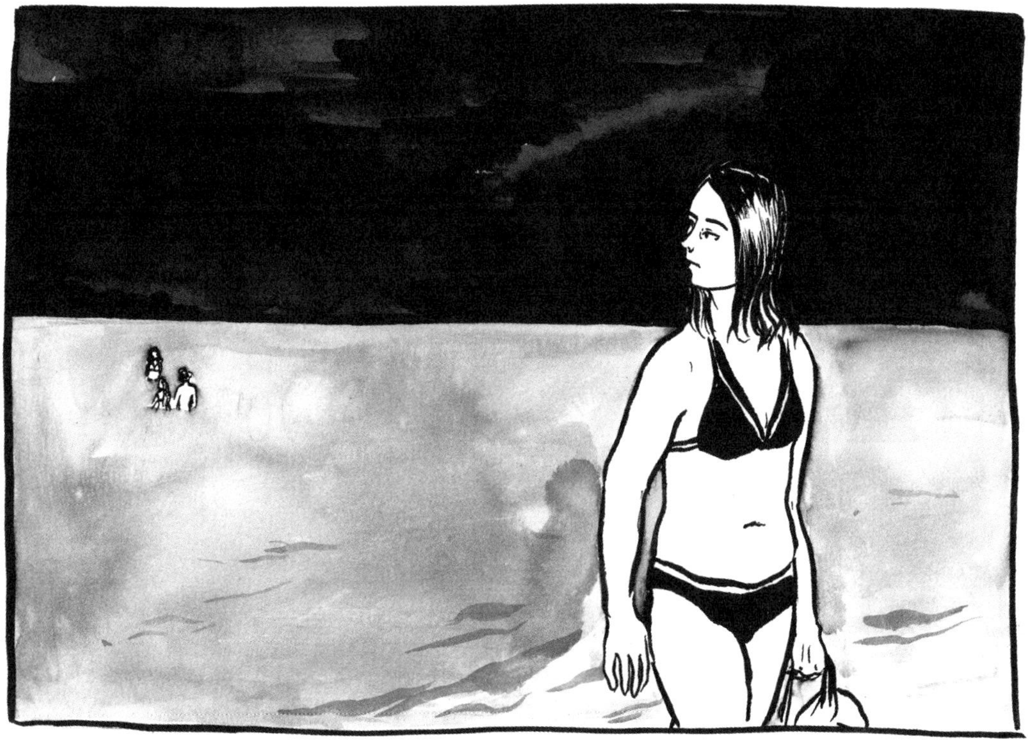

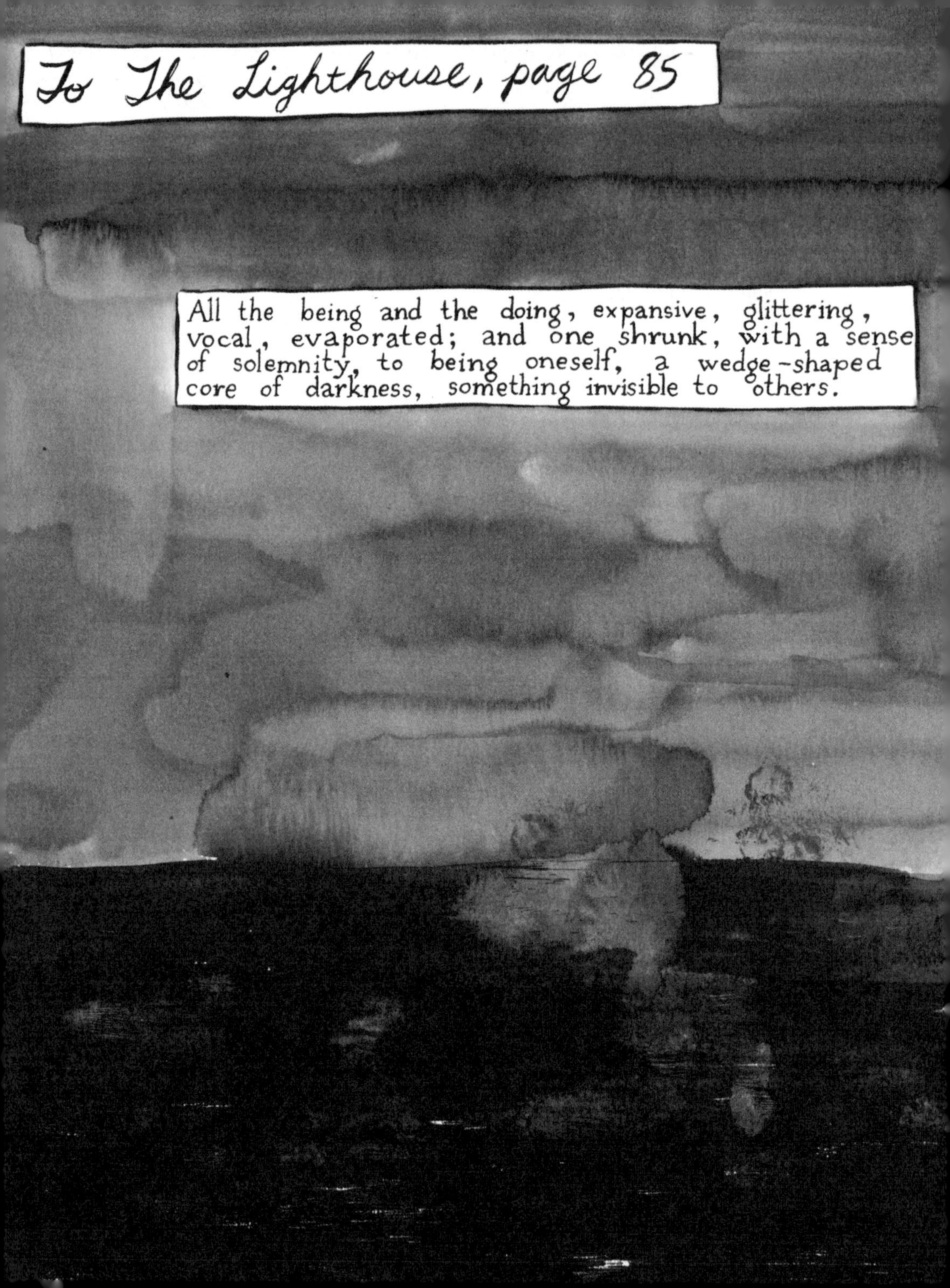
To The Lighthouse, page 85
All the being and the doing, expansive, glittering, vocal, evaporated; and one shrunk, with a sense of solemnity, to being oneself, a wedge-shaped core of darkness, something invisible to others.

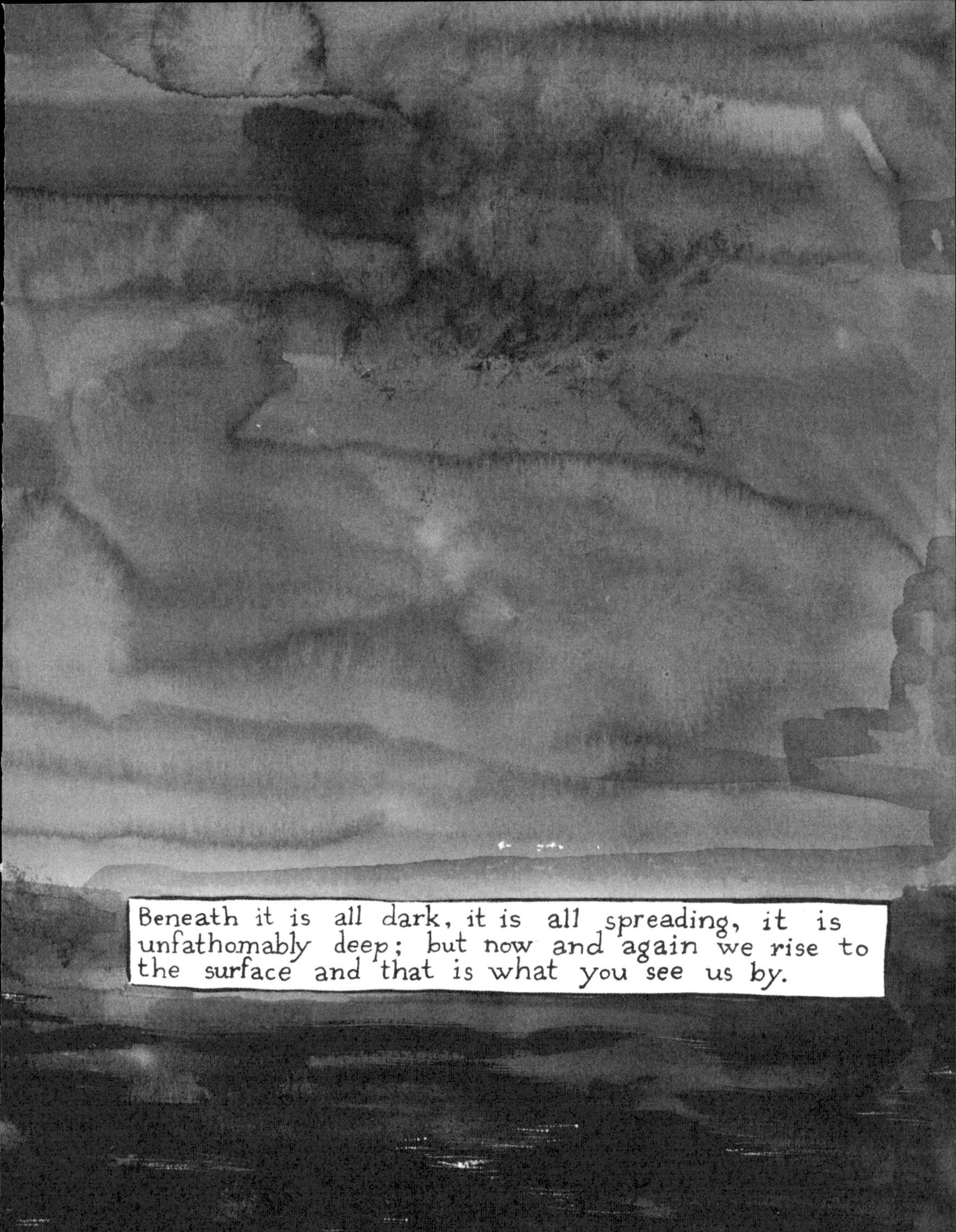
Beneath it is all dark, it is all spreading, it is unfathomably deep; but now and again we rise to the surface and that is what you see us by.

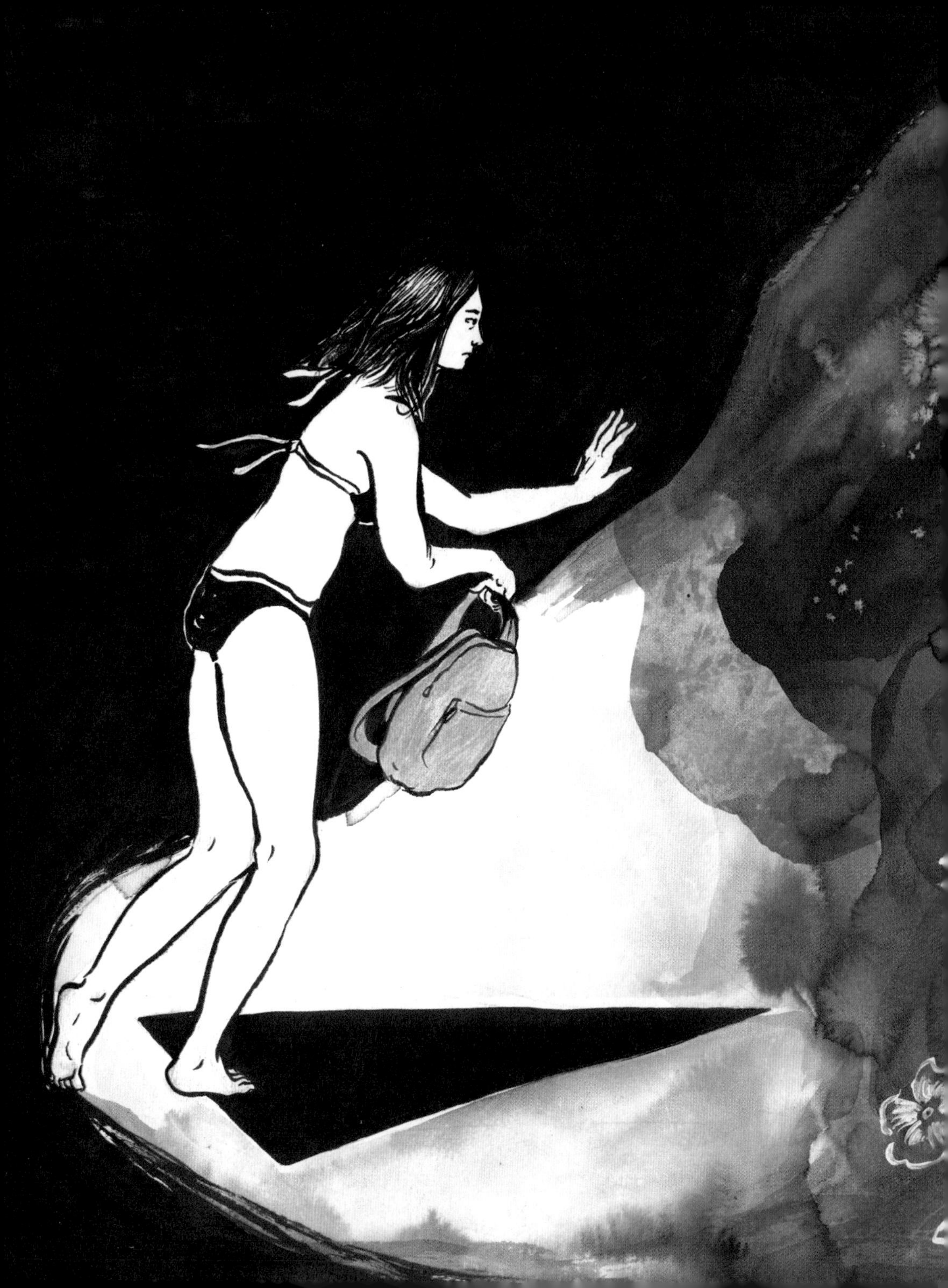

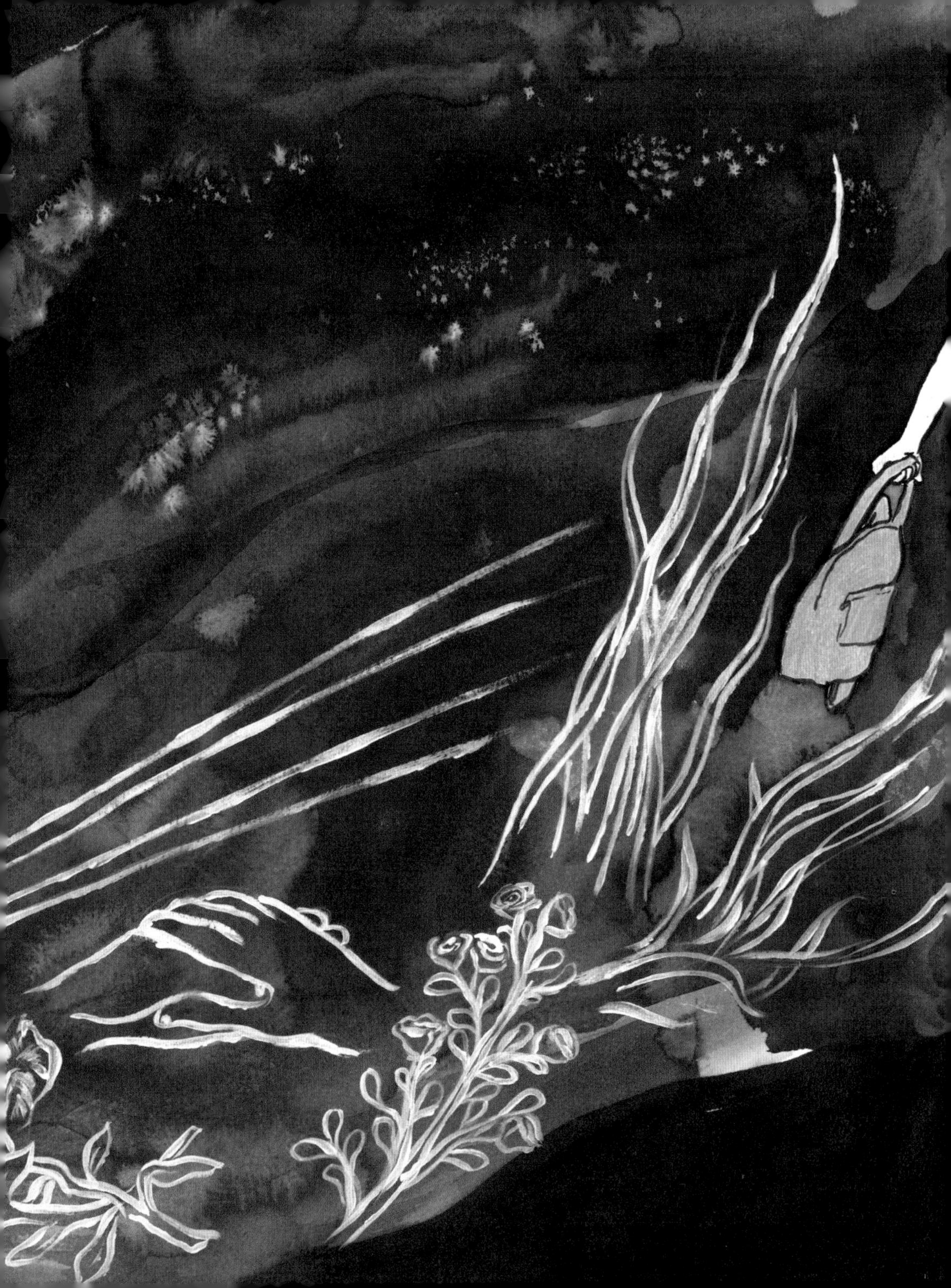

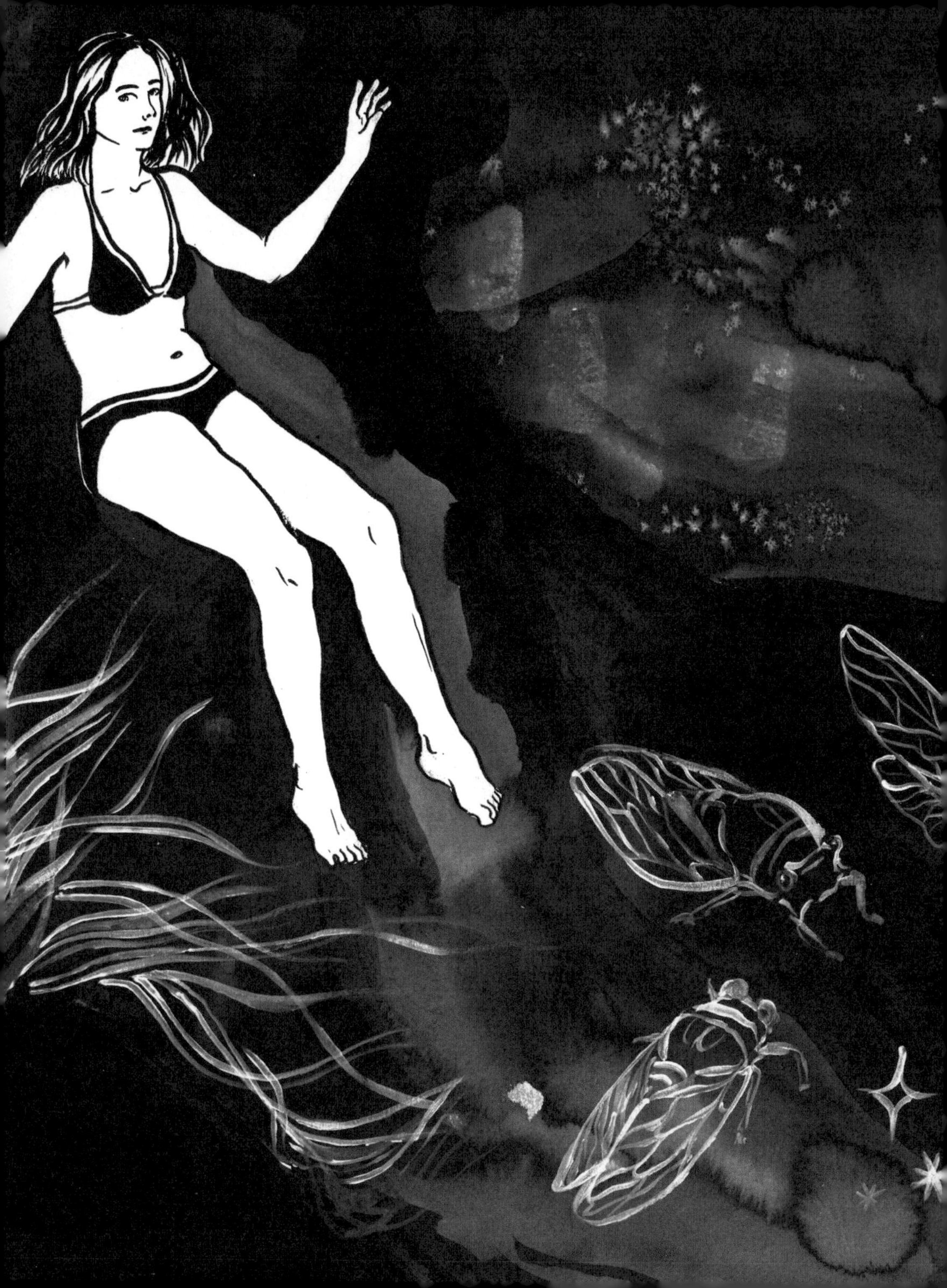

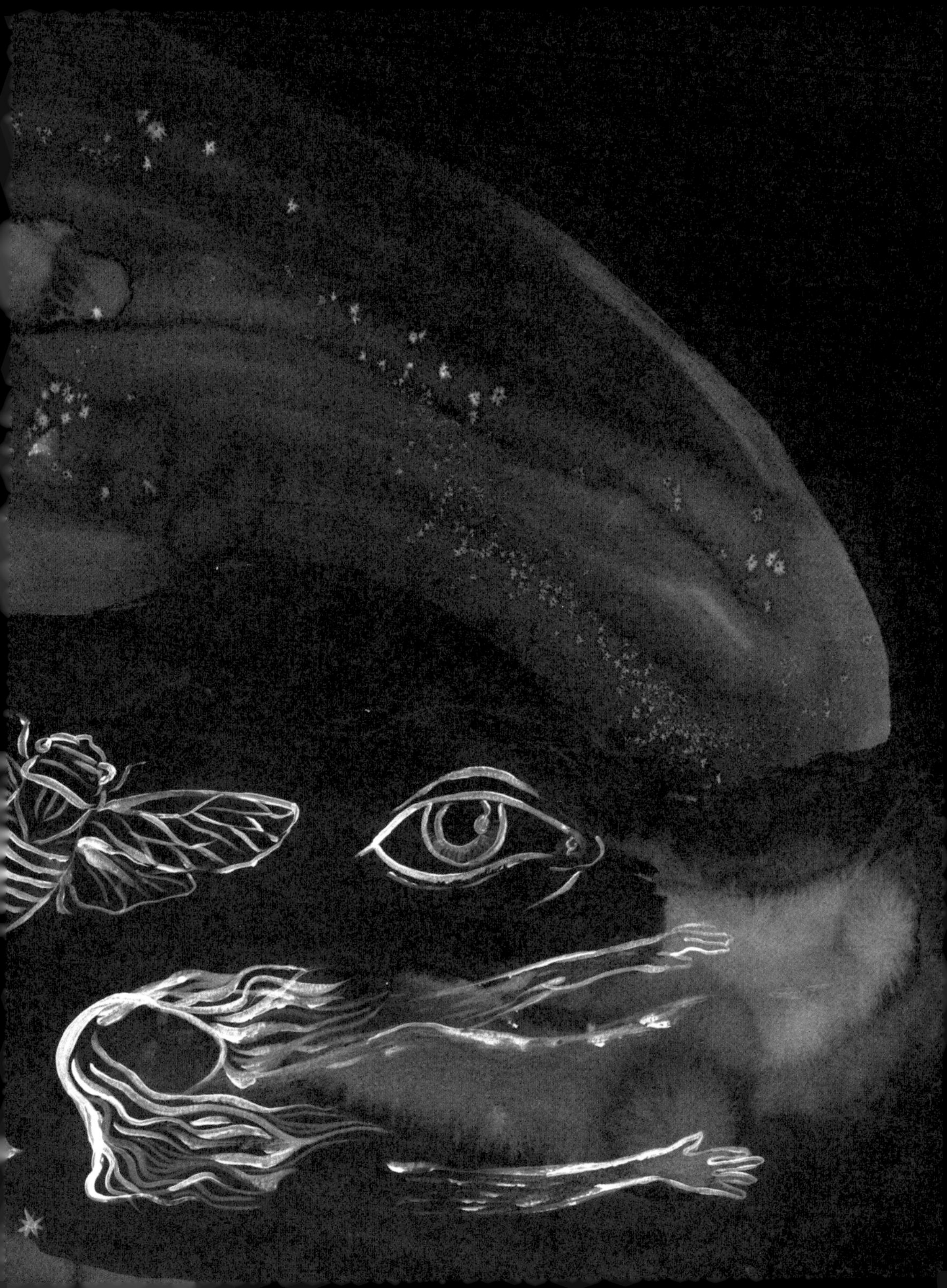

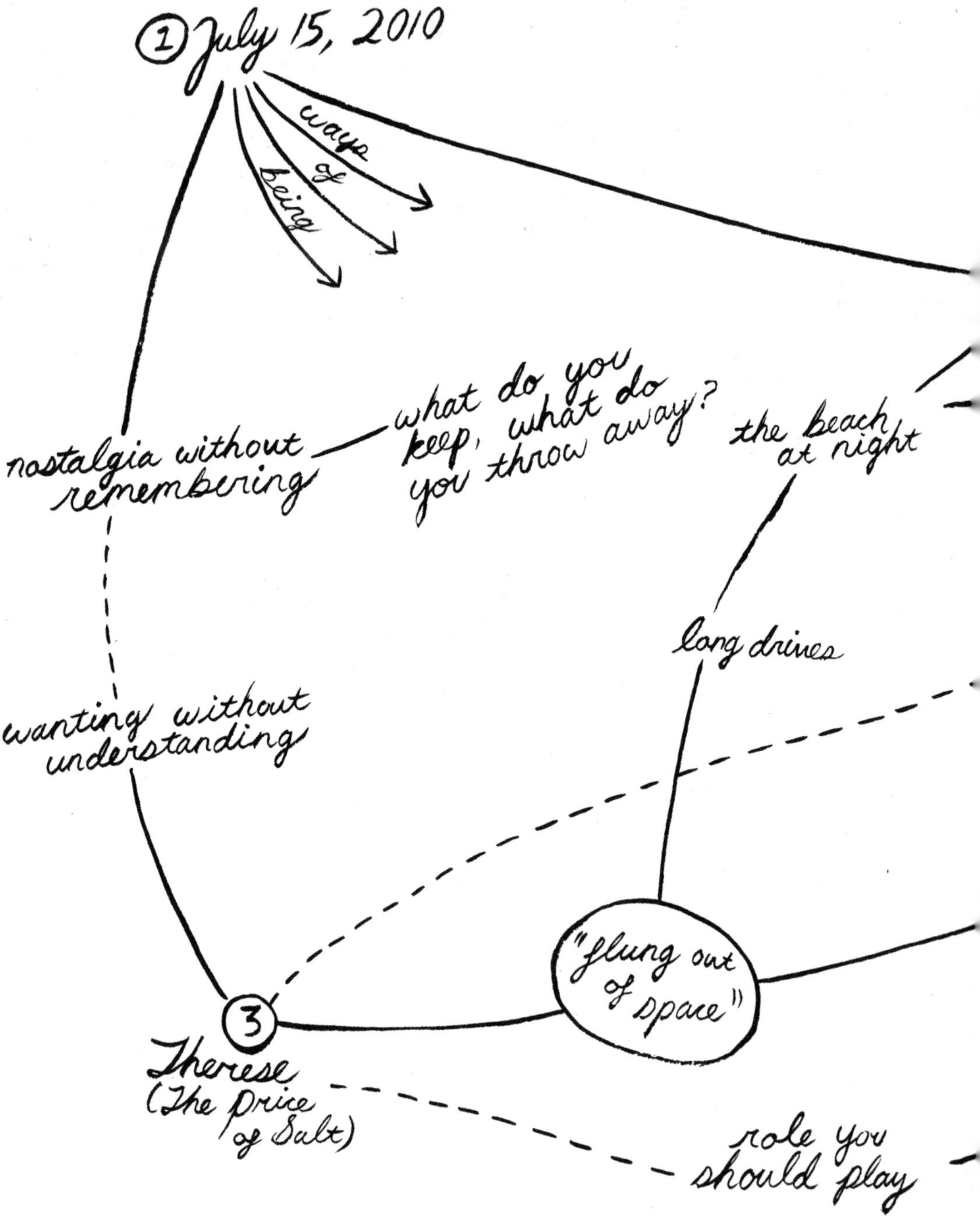

① July 15, 2010
ways of being
nostalgia without remembering
what do you keep, what do you throw away?
the beach at night
long drives
wanting without understanding
"flung out of space"
③ Therese (The Price of Salt)
role you should play

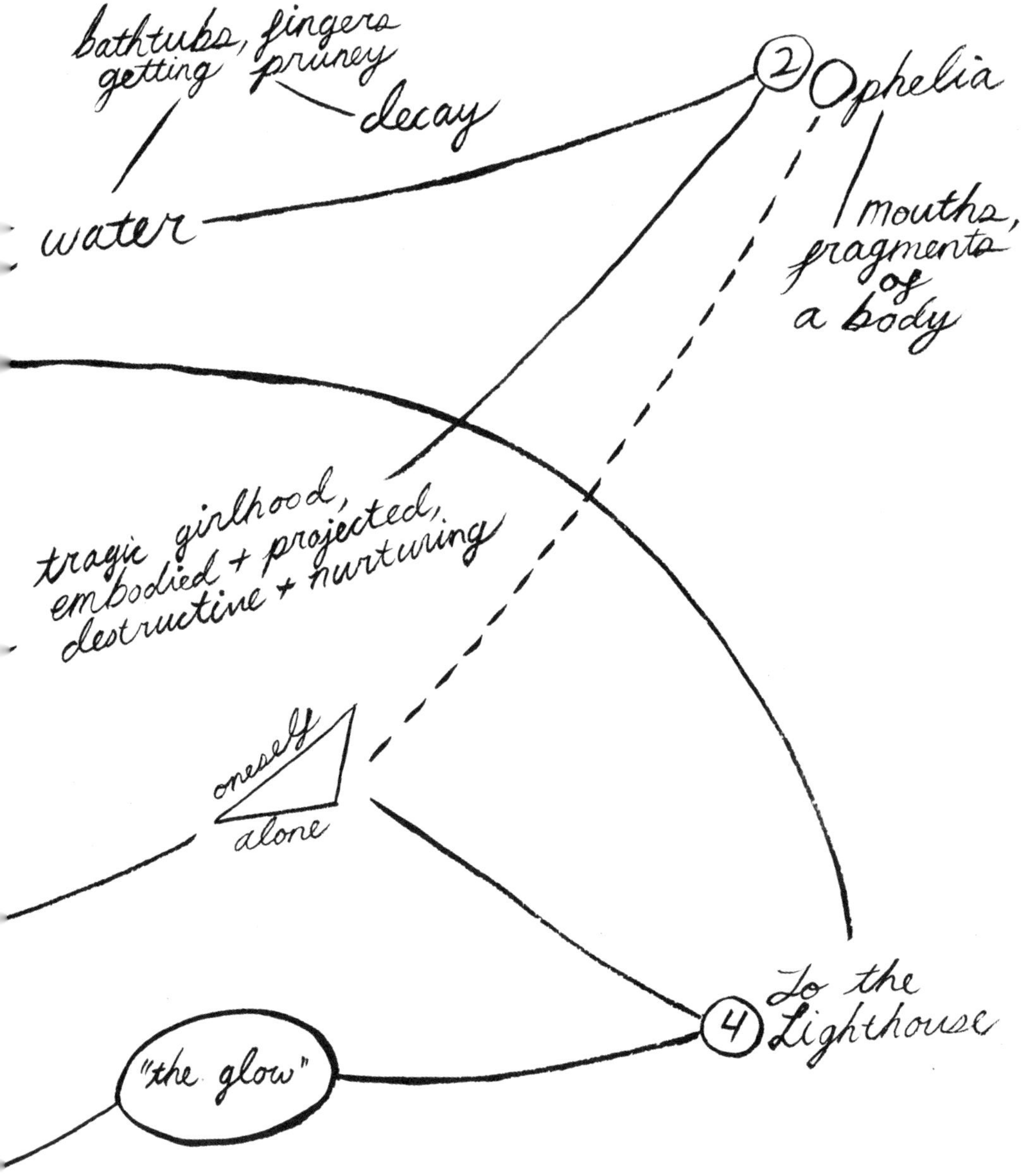
bathtubs, fingers getting pruney
decay
water
2 Ophelia
mouths, fragments of a body
tragic girlhood, embodied + projected, destructive + nurturing
oneself
alone
4 To the Lighthouse
"the glow"

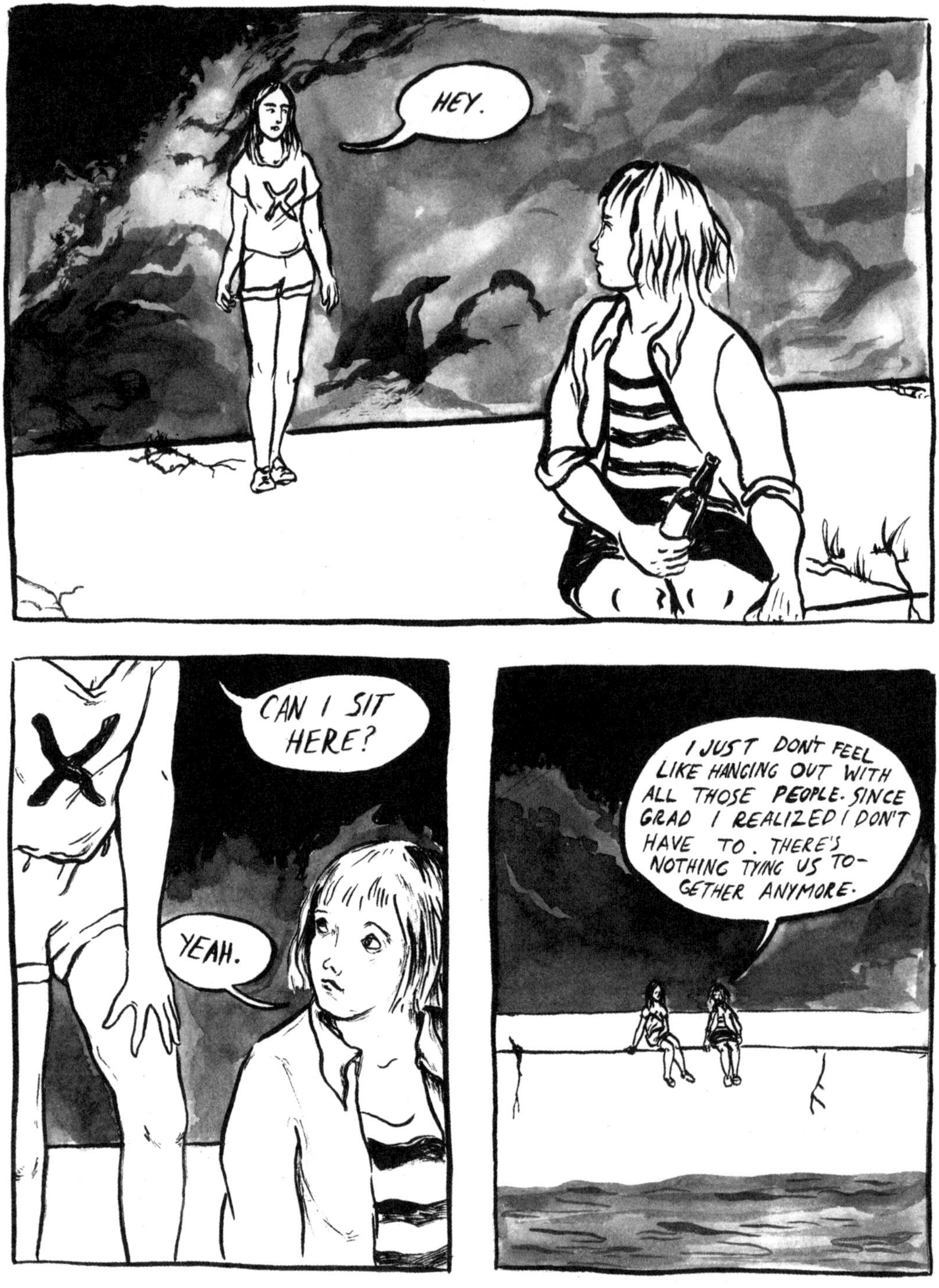
HEY.
CAN I SIT HERE?
YEAH.
I JUST DON'T FEEL LIKE HANGING OUT WITH ALL THOSE PEOPLE. SINCE GRAD I REALIZED I DON'T HAVE TO. THERE'S NOTHING TYING US TOGETHER ANYMORE.

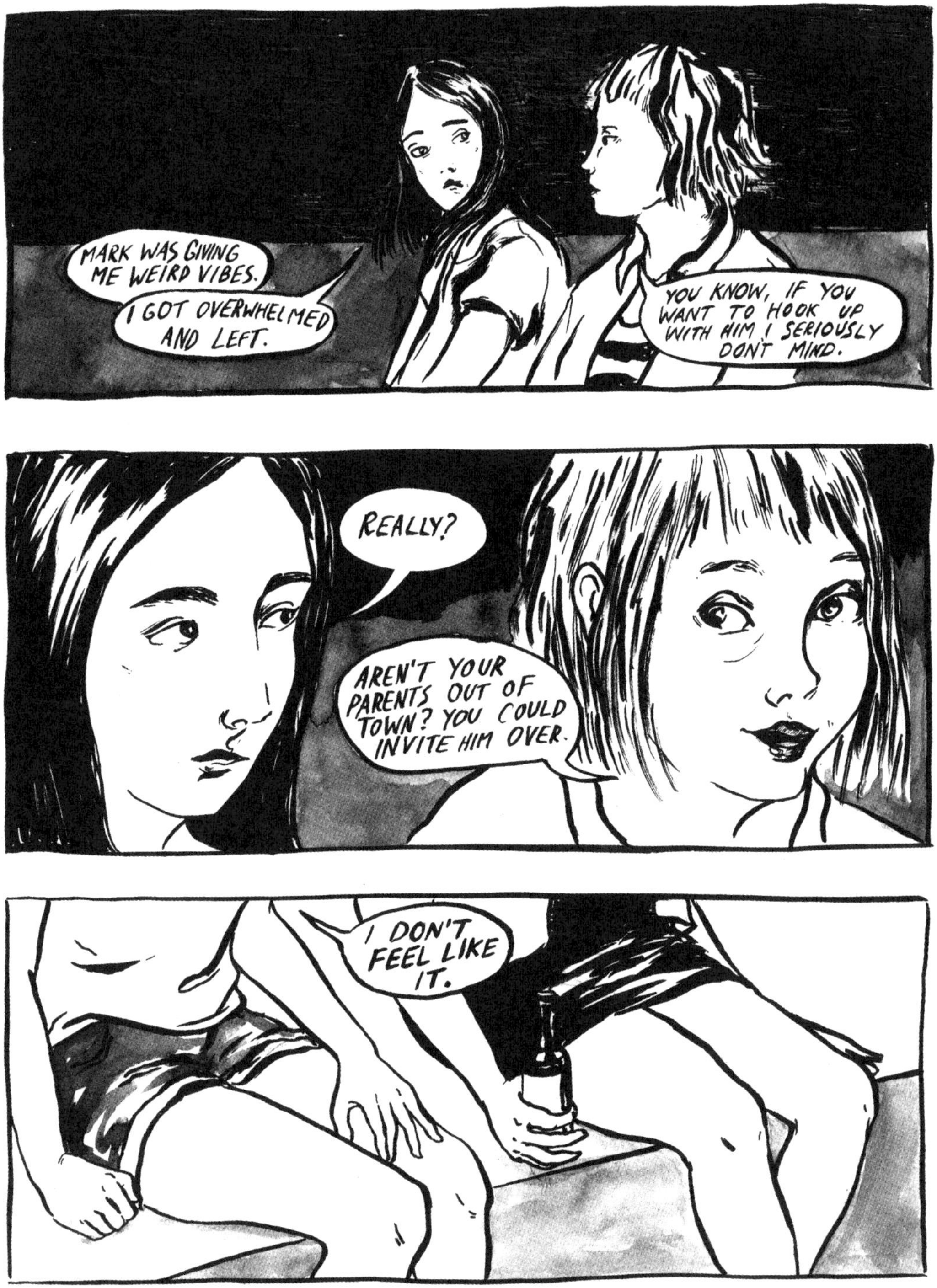
MARK WAS GIVING ME WEIRD VIBES.
I GOT OVERWHELMED AND LEFT.
YOU KNOW, IF YOU WANT TO HOOK UP WITH HIM I SERIOUSLY DON'T MIND.
REALLY?
AREN'T YOUR PARENTS OUT OF TOWN? YOU COULD INVITE HIM OVER.
I DON'T FEEL LIKE IT.

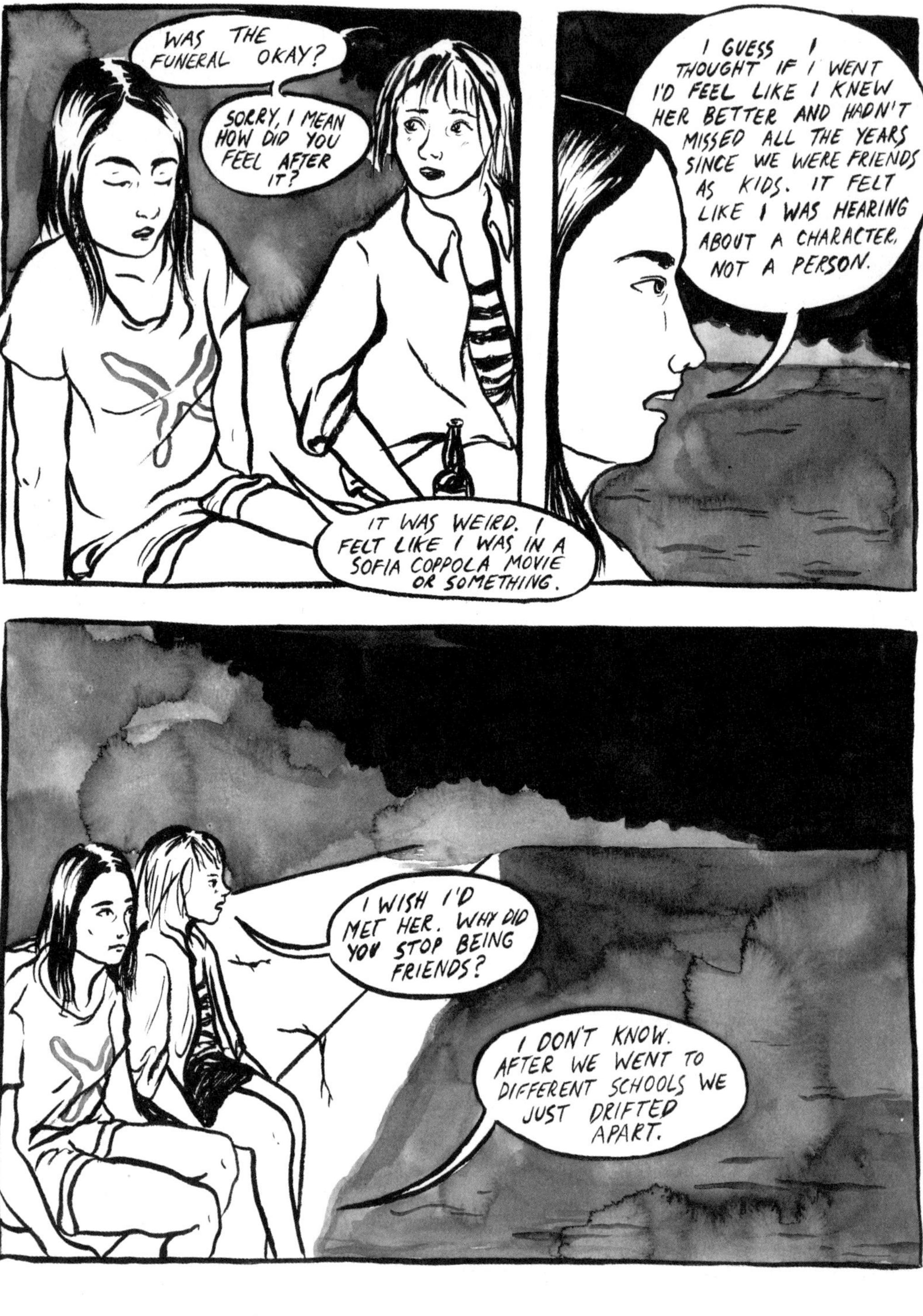
WAS THE FUNERAL OKAY?
SORRY, I MEAN HOW DID YOU FEEL AFTER IT?
IT WAS WEIRD. I FELT LIKE I WAS IN A SOFIA COPPOLA MOVIE OR SOMETHING.
I GUESS I THOUGHT IF I WENT I'D FEEL LIKE I KNEW HER BETTER AND HADN'T MISSED ALL THE YEARS SINCE WE WERE FRIENDS AS KIDS. IT FELT LIKE I WAS HEARING ABOUT A CHARACTER, NOT A PERSON.
I WISH I'D MET HER. WHY DID YOU STOP BEING FRIENDS?
I DON'T KNOW. AFTER WE WENT TO DIFFERENT SCHOOLS WE JUST DRIFTED APART.

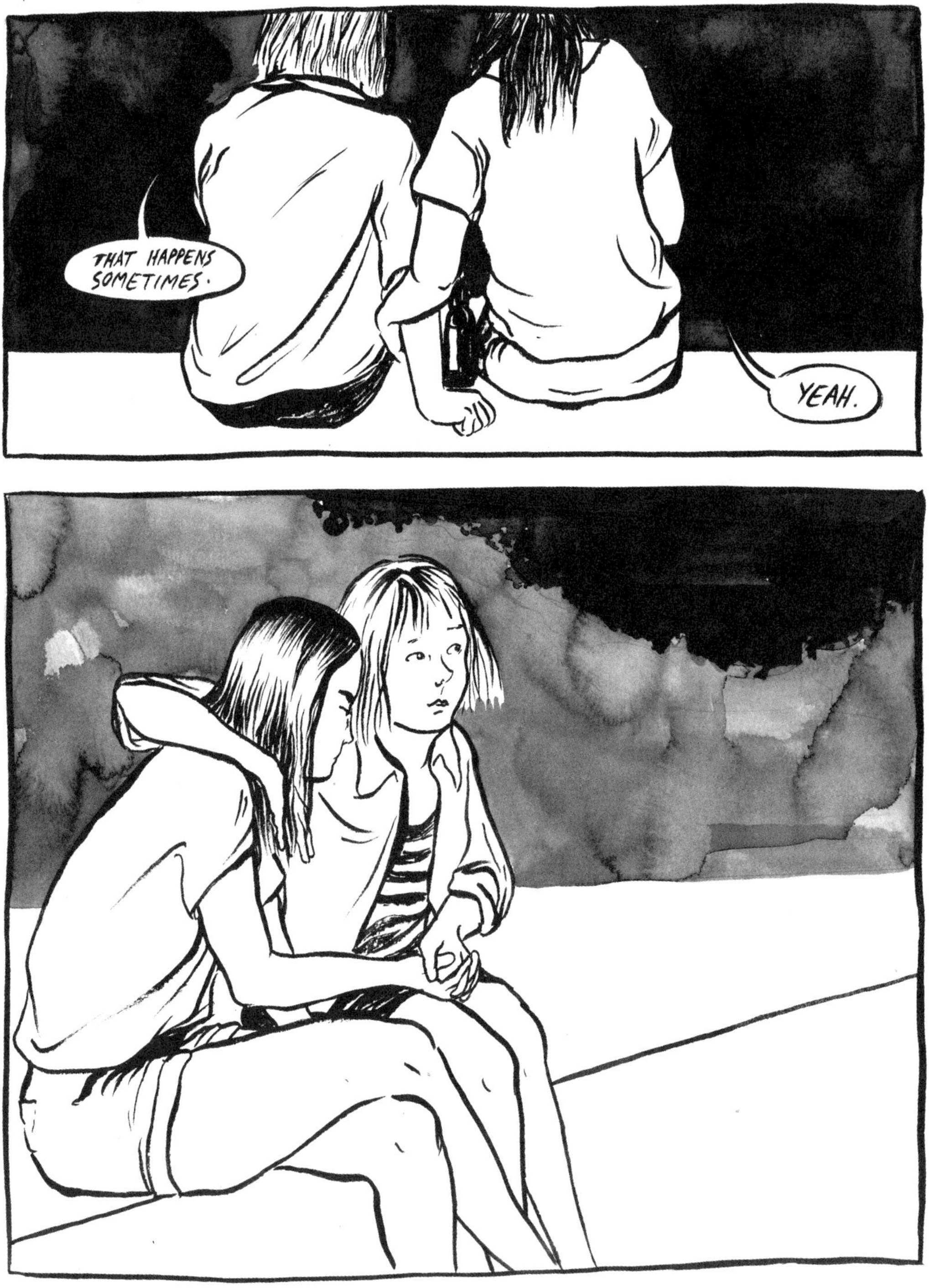
THAT HAPPENS SOMETIMES.
YEAH.

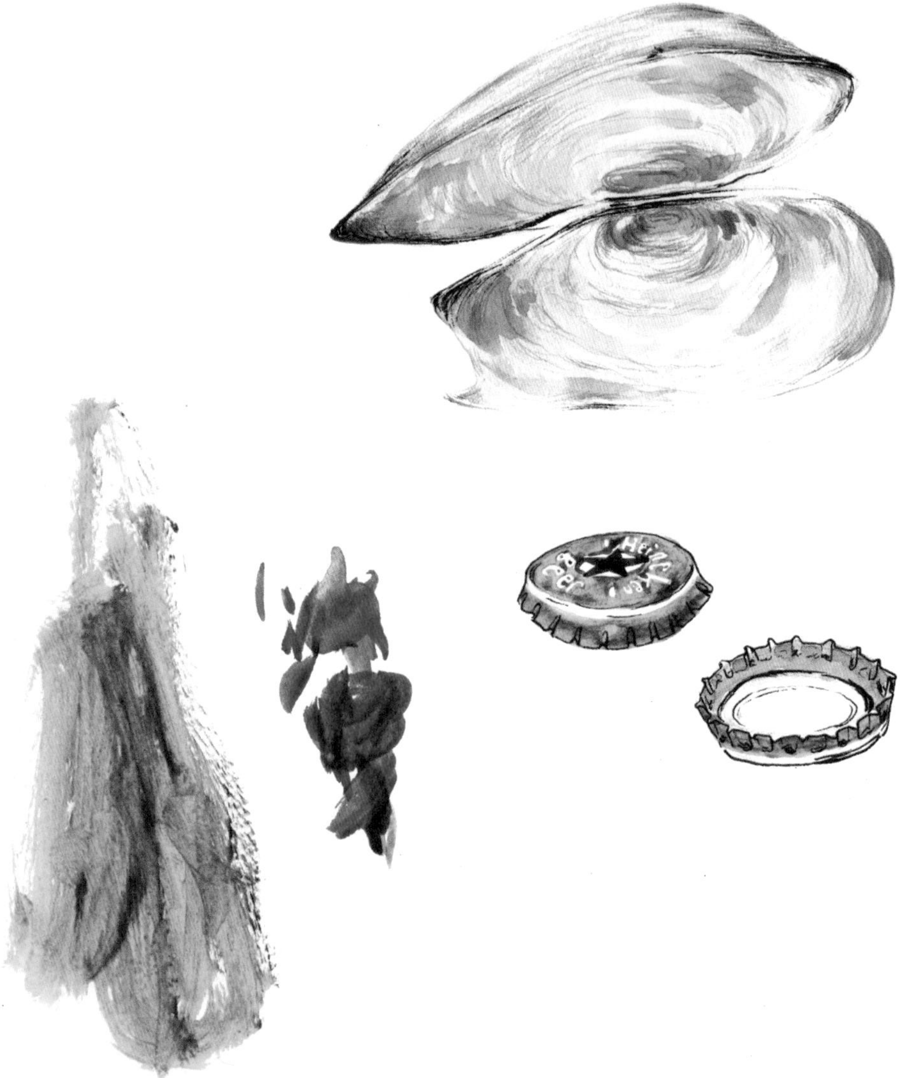
Heineken
Beer

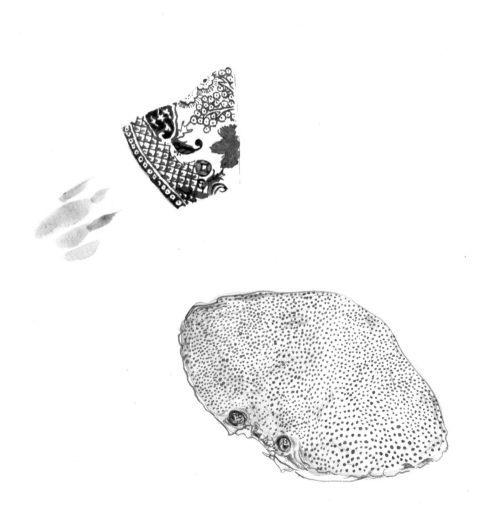

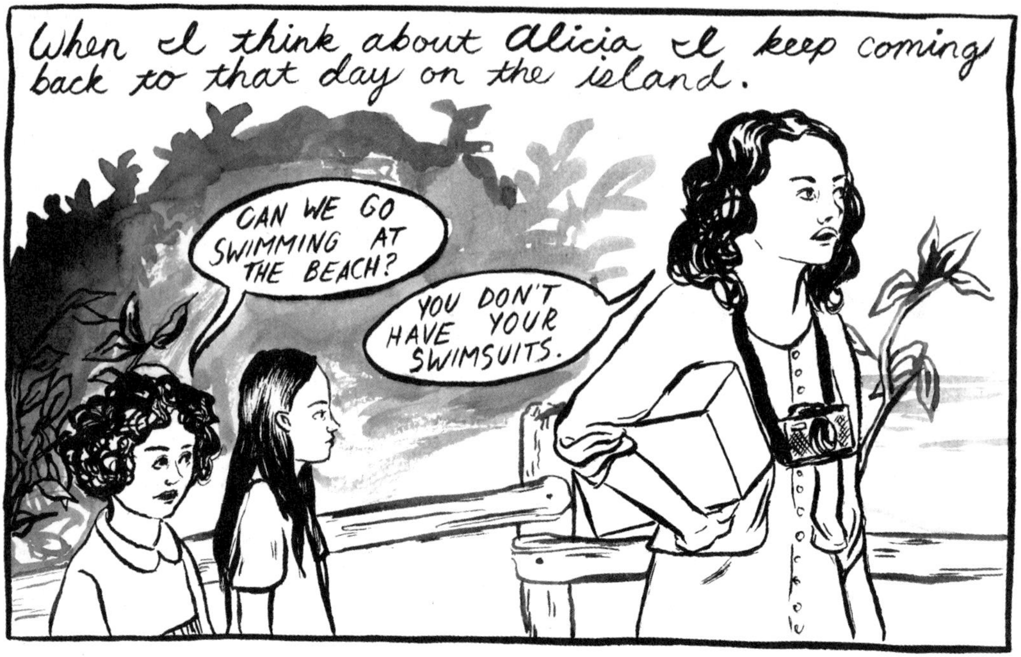
When I think about Alicia I keep coming back to that day on the island.
CAN WE GO SWIMMING AT THE BEACH?
YOU DON'T HAVE YOUR SWIMSUITS.

We were maybe seven or eight and her mom brought us to the beach to burn a shrine she'd built for her grand-mother out on the lake. In retrospect, I realize it was part of one of her art projects, but we were so small that to us it was just a thing happening.

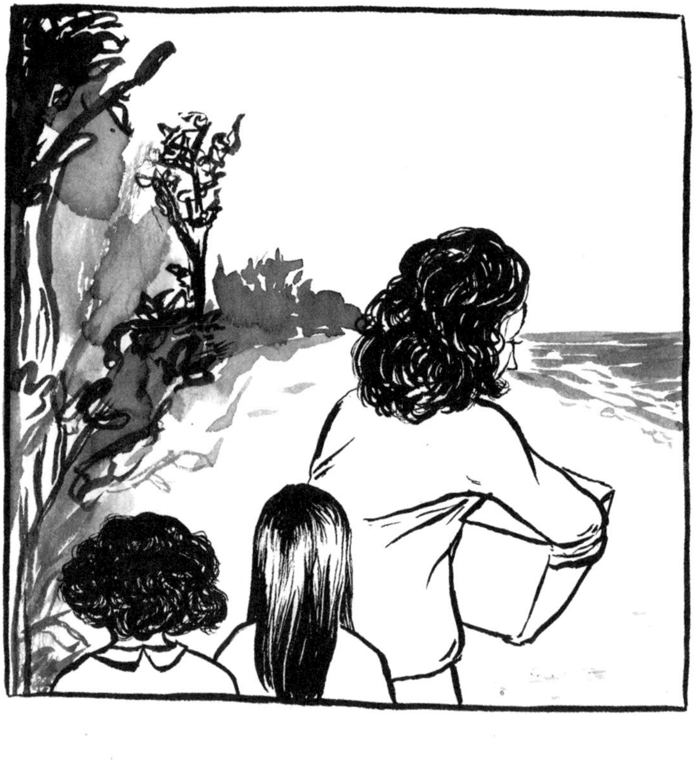

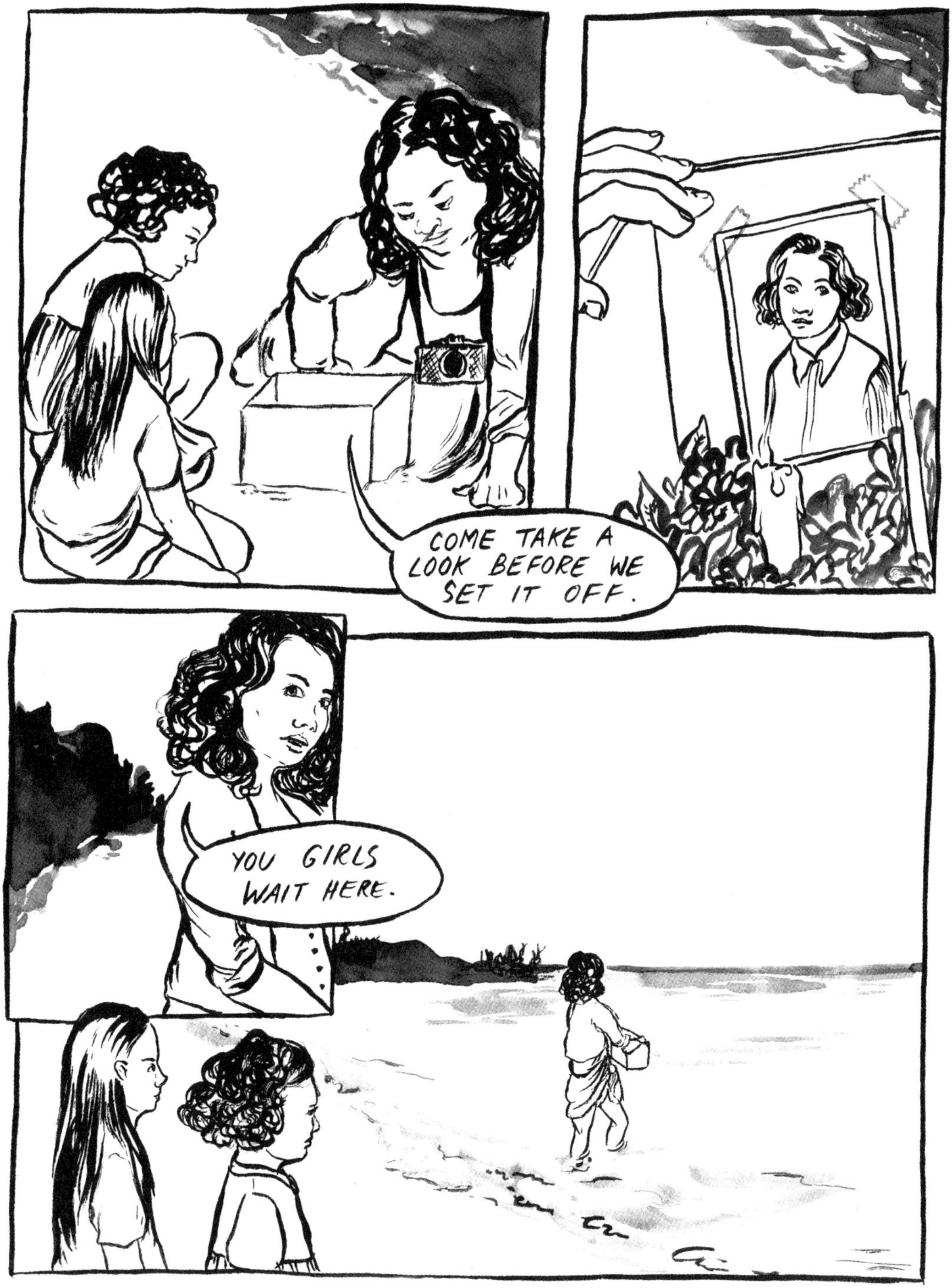
COME TAKE A LOOK BEFORE WE SET IT OFF.
YOU GIRLS WAIT HERE.

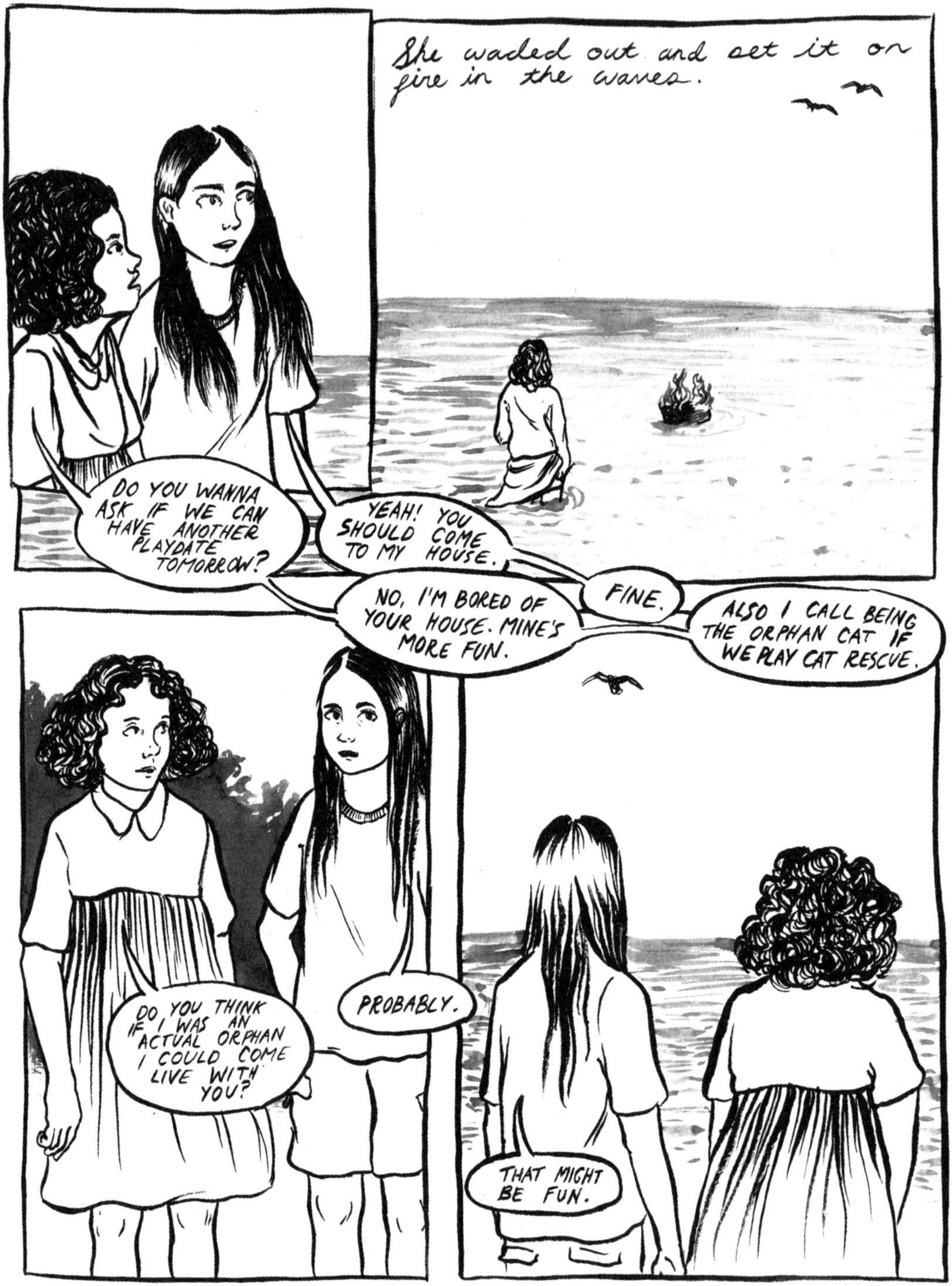
She waded out and set it on fire in the waves.
DO YOU WANNA ASK IF WE CAN HAVE ANOTHER PLAYDATE TOMORROW?
YEAH! YOU SHOULD COME TO MY HOUSE.
NO, I'M BORED OF YOUR HOUSE. MINE'S MORE FUN.
FINE.
ALSO I CALL BEING THE ORPHAN CAT IF WE PLAY CAT RESCUE.
DO YOU THINK IF I WAS AN ACTUAL ORPHAN I COULD COME LIVE WITH YOU?
PROBABLY.
THAT MIGHT BE FUN.

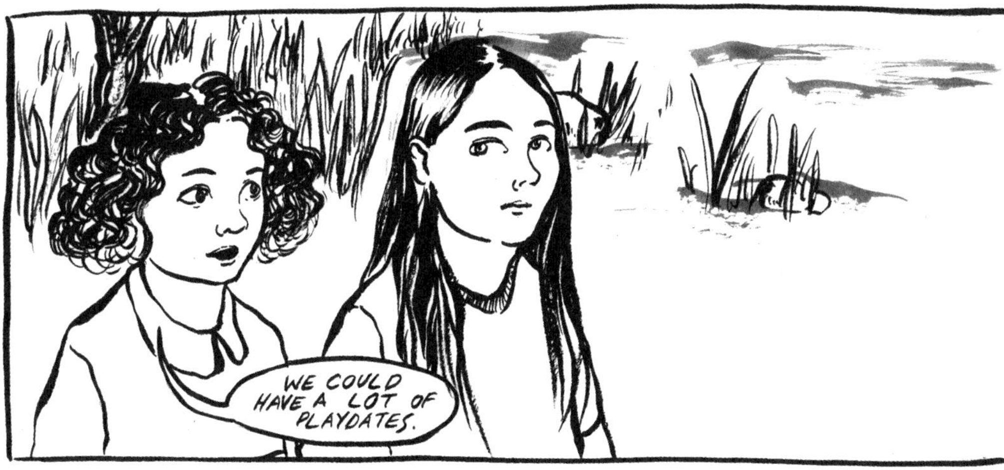
WE COULD HAVE A LOT OF PLAYDATES.

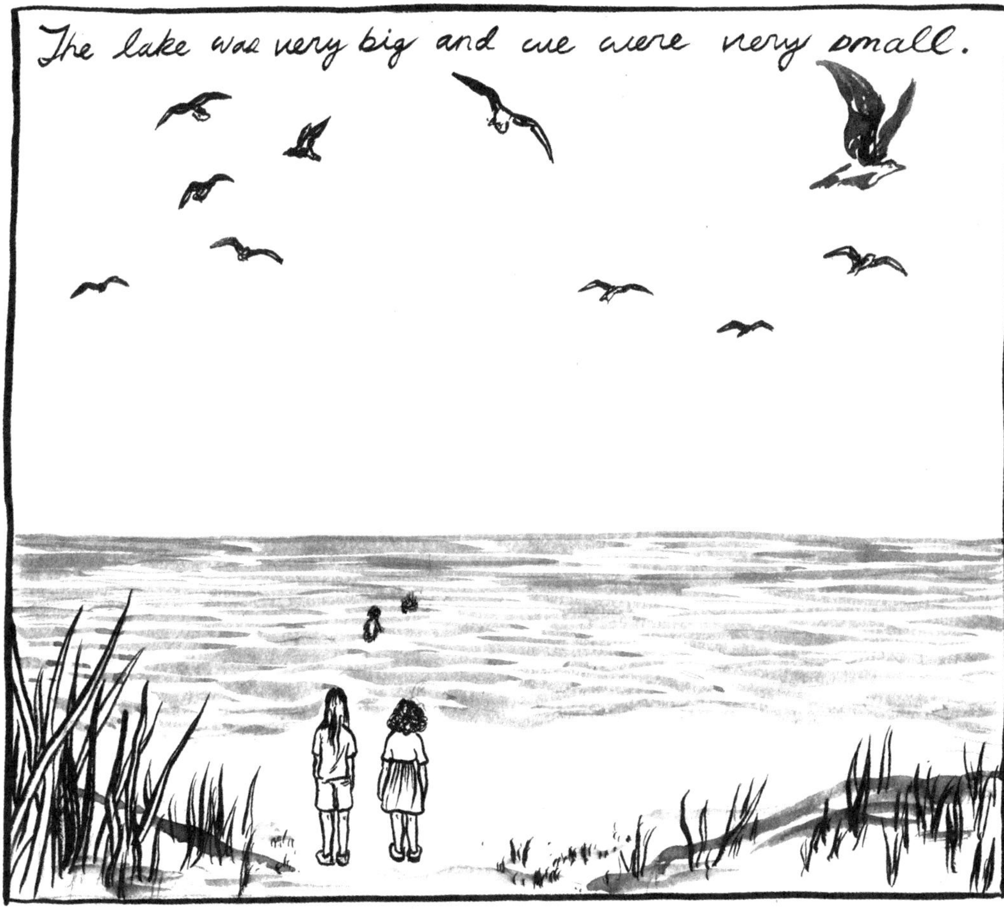
The lake was very big and we were very small.

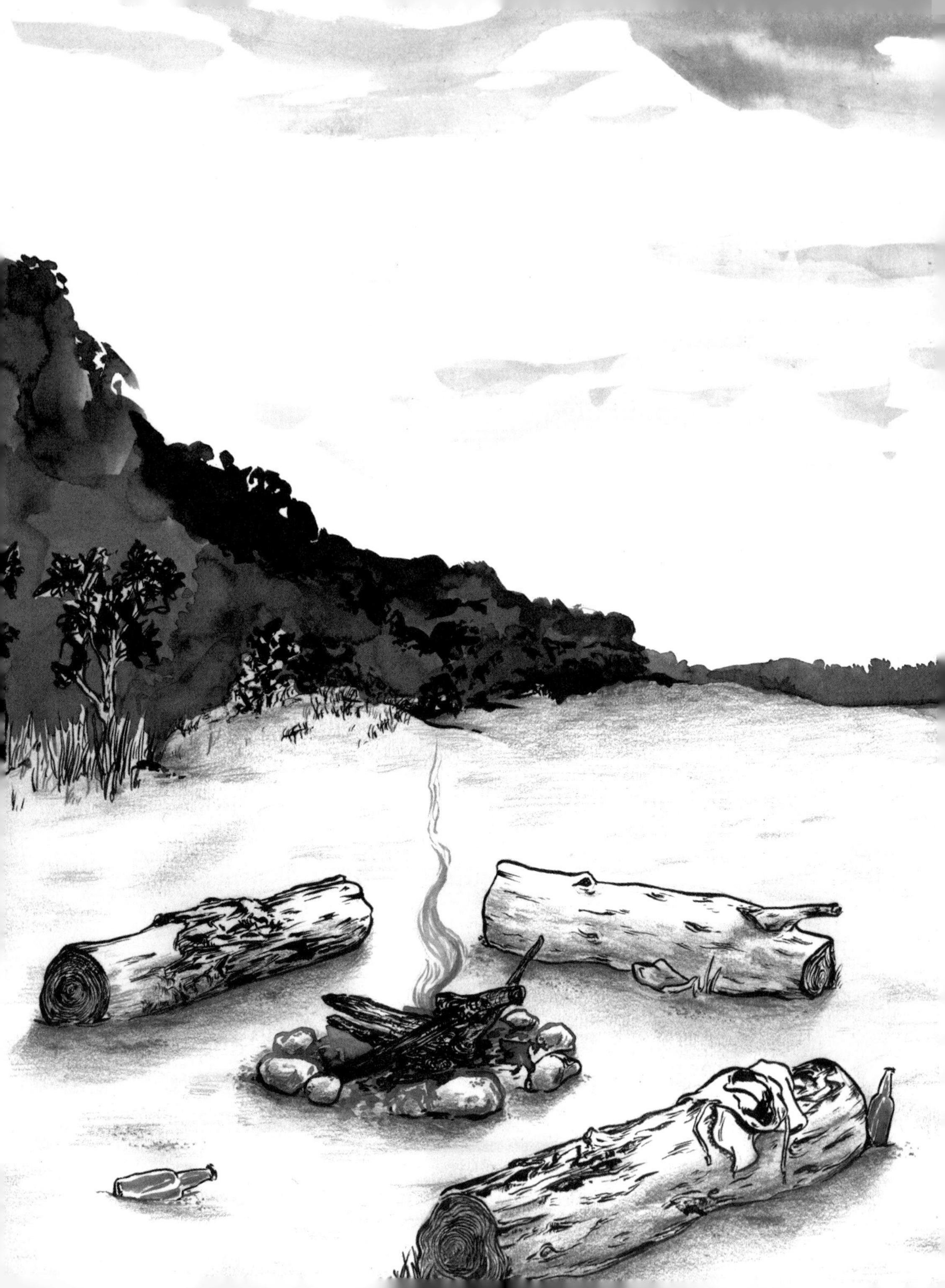

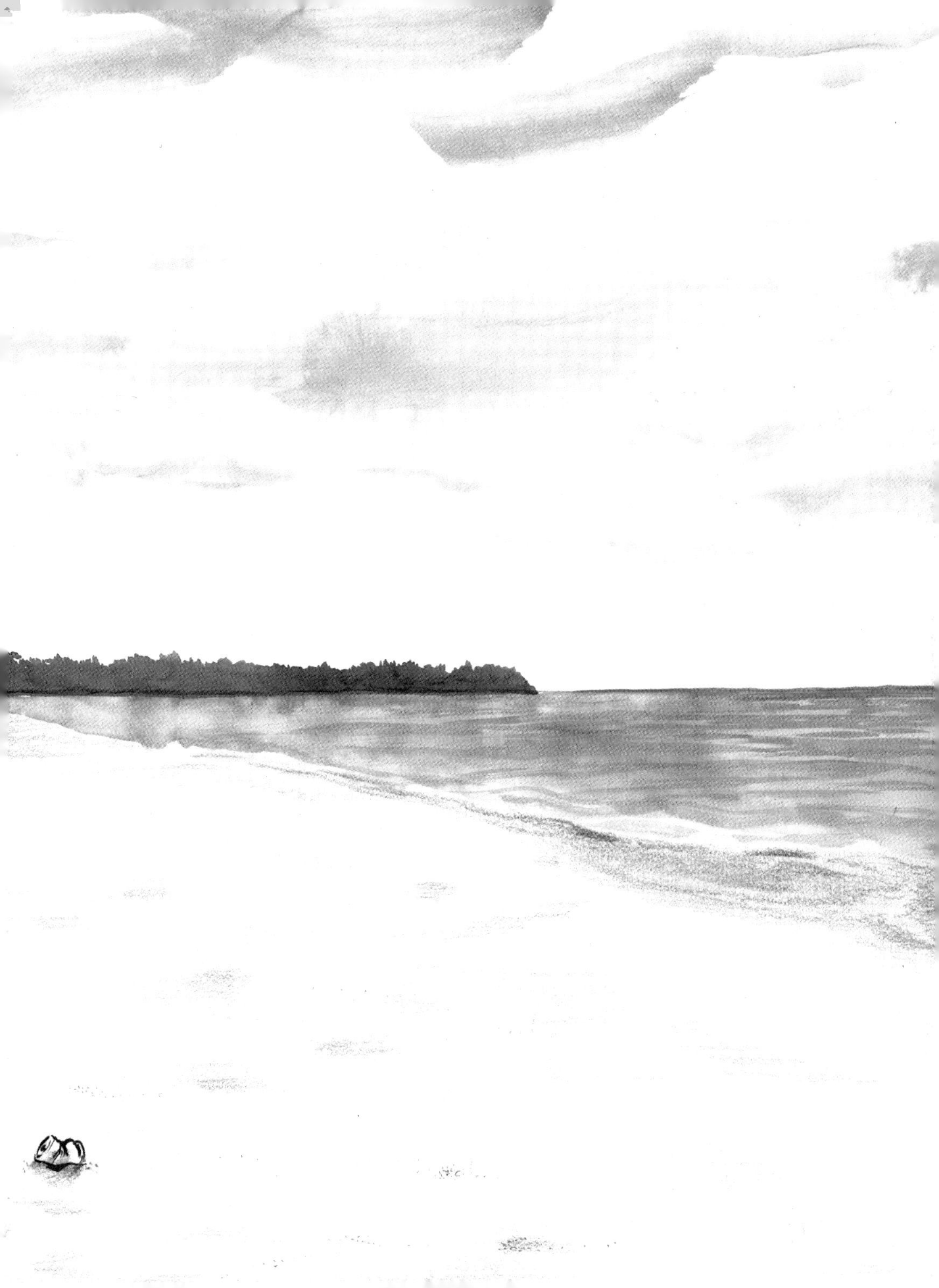

Zoe Maeve is a comics artist originally from Tkaronto/Toronto. In 2021 her first book, *The Gift*, was released with Conundrum Press and she was nominated for an Ignatz Award. She lives in Tiohtià:ke/Montreal with her partner and two black cats.